T0171673

ACCLAIM FOR ALESSANDRO BOFFA'S

You're an Animal, Viskovitz!

"It's [Boffa's] gift for turning scientific jargon into richly comic material . . . that makes his book such a Wild Kingdom of delight."
                    —*The New York Times Book Review*

"A cheeky little masterpiece that deserves its own plaque in the pantheon of comic literature."
                    —*San Francisco Chronicle*

"Charming. . . . [Boffa] brilliantly and often hilariously fuses animal biology with human frailty, narcissism, and egotism."   —*The Boston Sunday Globe*

"Wickedly funny. . . wildly inventive. . . . A terrific debut."   —*St. Petersburg Times*

"Exuberant, extravagant, and hilarious."
—*The Commercial Appeal*

"Wonderfully daffy. . . . As witty and entertaining as we've had from Italy since the death of Calvino."
—Alan Cheuse, *All Things Considered*

"An unmitigated delight. . . . A literary debut of promise, enchantment, and no small hilarity. It is always fiendishly clever and witty and often uproarious."
—*Buffalo News*

"A scientifically accurate, gleefully sexy, and philosophically mischievous improvisation on Ovid's *Metamorphosis*."
—*Booklist*

Alessandro Boffa

You're an Animal, Viskovitz!

Alessandro Boffa was born in Moscow. He completed his studies in biology in Rome, and now divides his time between Italy and Thailand. This is his first book.

INTERNATIONAL

You're an Animal, Viskovitz!

You're an Animal, Viskovitz!

Viskovitz!

ALESSANDRO BOFFA

———————

*Translated from the Italian by John Casey,
with Maria Sanminiatelli*

———————

Illustrated by Roz Chast

VINTAGE INTERNATIONAL • VINTAGE BOOKS
A DIVISION OF RANDOM HOUSE, INC. • NEW YORK

FIRST VINTAGE INTERNATIONAL EDITION, JUNE 2003

Translation copyright © 2002 by Alfred A. Knopf, a division of Random House, Inc.

All rights reserved under International and Pan-American Copyright
Conventions. Published in the United States by Vintage Books, a division
of Random House, Inc., New York, and simultaneously in Canada by
Random House of Canada Limited, Toronto. Originally published in
Italy as *Sei una bestia, Viskovitz* by Edizioni Garzanti, s.p.a., Milan, in 1998.
Copyright © 1998 Edizioni Garzanti, s.p.a. This translation originally
published in hardcover in the United States by Alfred A. Knopf,
a division of Random House, Inc., New York, in 2002.

Vintage is a registered trademark and Vintage International and
colophon are trademarks of Random House, Inc.

The Library of Congress has cataloged the Knopf edition as follows:
Boffa, Alessandro.
[Sei una bestia, Viskovitz, English]
You're an animal, Viskovitz / Alessandro Boffa : translated from the Italian
by John Casey with Maria Sanminiatelli.
p. cm.
ISBN 0-375-40528-3
I. Casey, John. II. Sanminiatelli, Maria. III. Title.
PQ4862.O338.S4513 2002
853'.914—dc21
2001050592

Vintage ISBN: 978-0-375-70483-3

Author photograph © Sybil Mostert
Illustrations by Roz Chast
Book design by Suvi Asch

www.vintagebooks.com

For Sybil

CONTENTS

CONTENTS

You're an Animal, Viskovitz!

PROLOGUE

So there we were on that ice floe, just the two of us, adrift in the polar night. Viskovitz turned and said, "I'd like you to get our conversation down in black and white."

"It's not possible," I answered. "I'm not a typist. I'm not a writer. I'm a penguin. As far as I'm concerned, 'getting it down in black and white' means making more penguins."

So instead there I was a month later, standing still with an egg under my belly, remembering . . .

I was the one who had brought up the subject.

How's Life Treating You, Viskovitz?

There's nothing more boring than life, nothing more depressing than light, nothing more bogus than reality. For me every waking was a dying—living was being dead.

Jana squeaked, "Wake up, Visko! It's May! They'll end up getting all the best acorns."

With great difficulty I stretched and grudgingly opened one eye. Because in spite of everything, you have to live.

"Just a minute," I croaked. "I have to thaw out."

It was the end of an eight-month hibernation. I was waking up in the gray hereafter, the underworld of dormice.

In the darkness of the den I made out topiform shadows tottering past piles of slumberers, heading out of this sepulcher—souls of those who had passed on, who were transmigrating into wakefulness. As was I.

I rolled onto one side, and all the bones of my mortal remains creaked. I began to recognize the familiar outlines of members of my tribe—nephews, nieces, grandnephews and grandnieces, grandparents and great-grandparents, parents and parents-in-law. Some of them were catching forty more winks, curled up under their long furry tails. They were groaning as they gave themselves over to that devastating pleasure.

As my metabolism got into gear I was tortured by pains in my joints, by dehydration, by the distress of every single cell. It was the agony of reawakening, of a torment that would last another four months until the next hibernation. At a time like this there's only hunger that gives you the strength to get to your feet—the knowledge that if you don't fatten up, you won't be able to get back to sleep.

"Up and at 'em!" I said to myself. "At your age you can reasonably expect another three hibernations. And it would be a shame, old dormouse, to miss out on them."

Like a zombie, I hoisted up my body—worn out, wooden, deprived of fats and spirit—and shoved it awkwardly in the direction of the light. My eyes watered in the glare.

"You're thin as a pin, Visko," Jana shouted at me.

"Come on—let's go gather acorns." For years she'd been the mate to whom I'd been faithful, not out of any monogamous inclination—which we dormice frankly do not have—but out of laziness and a desire to be bored. She was the ugliest and most depressing female of the whole community, the silliest and most tedious. I'd chosen her for exactly that. Because only a life made up of boredom and frustration leads to fulfilling and magnificent dreams. And those are the moments that count. If the hereafter— that is, wakefulness—is hell, then life—that is, dreaming—will be paradise. Not the other way around.

I didn't feel like venturing out in the branches, so I spied a couple of acorns that had landed on the ground and, at a prudently slow pace, lowered myself along the trunk. I staggered up to one of the nuts, tore off the cap with my paws and sank my molars into the ripe cotyledon. I immediately felt better.

My den was the former nest of a woodpecker hollowed out of a sessiliflore oak. We'd been passing it down in our family for generations. It bore the most fruit of any tree in the woods; all it took to make it to the fall was to pick it clean. My children were already working at it, idly stretched out in the branches. With paternal satisfaction I appreciated their indolent lounging, their dull eyes, their stubborn resistance to life. Then I set off toward the lakeshore.

Because another thing you have to do while you're awake, besides putting on some fat and trying to bore

yourself, is to store up oneiric material for the next hibernation. For this we dormice always make the rounds of
the most enchanting places. We're looking for inspiration
for our stories—characters, incidents. There is yet another
way of enriching your imagination, and that is to listen to
someone else's dreams, hoping to find in them some idea
you can copy. That's what Zucotic, Petrovic and Lopez
were doing as they sprawled in a patch of sun under an
oak, sweeping up fallen acorns with their tails.

"Good to see you up, Viskovitz," Lopez said. "So tell us
how it went."

I cut him off. "Talking wears me out."

There was nothing I could learn from them. Lopez's
dreams were horror stories in which everyone ended up
in the fangs of a weasel or an otter. In Petrovic's, on the
other hand, there were dormice who killed everyone only
to end up getting killed by Petrovic himself, one after
another, bite by bite. Zucotic, poor guy, suffered from
insomnia. If you heard a voice coming from the other
world while you were sleeping, it was always him.

My own dreams weren't ones you could talk about
in public. They were always about a certain female
dormouse, and I can assure you it wasn't Jana. A she-
dormouse who exists only in dreams—the masterpiece of
my imagination. It had taken me years of ugliness and
frustration to succeed in imagining that absolute perfection of murine features, that exact combination of sanc-
tity and sin. I had made her as beautiful as sleep, as
seductive as a yawn, as soft as a pillow.

And I named her Ljuba.

Thinking of her always gave me an abrupt and deep desire to sleep. I took three more steps and collapsed next to a tree trunk, out for the count . . .

I found her where I'd left her, in the tropical forest I'd dreamed for her, among hibiscus flowers in the shade of acacias, that fairyland habitat where there are no noises, only music; no odors, only perfume; no uphill, only downhill. There was nothing to poke you and nothing hard to bump into. Everything, even the tree trunks, was lined with furs, flower petals and feathers. There were no predators or rivals. There was no male besides me, and there was no other god but Viskovitz.

I greeted her with a *zi-zi,* our dormouse love-call. Then, coming down from a banana tree, I approached, gorgeous and indolent as a rodent god.

"I'm back, my love," I squeaked. "I'm here only for you."

"Right now I have things to do, Visko," she said, sighing. "I'm looking for an oak tree. It's not easy finding an acorn or a beechnut in the middle of these banana trees."

"You have only to ask," I told her, and with a single act of my imagination I made three acorns pop out of the ground, big as watermelons, without any cap and without any husk. Like all enlightened dormice, I knew how to dream while being conscious of dreaming. That made each of these instants immensely richer.

"But now, my treasure, come take care of me," I ordered. "I don't have a whole hibernation to play around with, just a little nap. Look at that bed of blossoms, it seems to me an ideal place . . ."

"No, Visko."

"No?"

It isn't pleasant to hear someone say no to you in your own dream. Notwithstanding the progress I'd made in training my oneiric creativity, I hadn't yet succeeded in subjecting to my control a strong character such as I'd given Ljuba. She gave me no rest.

"I'm tired of being treated like a little doll and obeying your whims," she snorted, shaking her whiskers. "It's easy for you. For you this is only a dream, and you can do anything you want with it. For me it's the only life I have—I want you to let me live it . . ."

"You know it's not your only life—you know I'll bring you back to life in every dream I'll have."

"Sure, they all say that. Meanwhile, you don't give me the time to eat or express a thought. You make me live in this ridiculous soporific world of yours, without dormice, without oak trees, in this eternal dusk. You don't let me have babies, you don't let me have a life of my own . . ."

"But I let you dream . . ."

"Oh, right—but what can I dream if all I know is this fairy-tale world of yours?"

"Let's not argue about it now, my treasure, I really have just a little time. Cheer up and come over here."

"No, Visko."

As usual, it ended up that to make her feel "alive," as

she called it, I had to dream all the vulgarities of life for her: sunrise, oaks, beeches, and maybe even Zucotic. I was more tired than when I fell asleep. It took at least an hour for Ljuba to come close enough to me to let me feel the touch of her sweet-smelling fur. Then she slowly stretched out on the moss in a come-hither way and mewed two provocative *zi-zis*.

"No, Ljuba," I warned her. "You know that's not what I want."

The problem with Ljuba was that she never wanted to do with me those things that boy and girl dormice do in dreams—that is, sleep. To share the magic moment of nodding off, the wickedness of yawning, the passion of dozing, the final fusion of bodies in one devastating slumber, the fusion of souls in a single triumphant dream.

When she was with me, she wanted to gather nuts, make love, have children and all those banalities. But at the crucial moment, just when her eyelids were beginning to close, she always refused to let herself go. So it always ended with my having to do without that perfect pleasure, and this time, too, seemed it wasn't going to be any different.

But she started by saying, "Okay, Visko. I want to make you happy. Let's do it. This time it suits me, too."

I couldn't believe my ears.

Suddenly I felt a paw on my neck and I woke up. I was understandably furious. If I'd had the strength I would have been capable of murder. Anyone who wakes you up doesn't deserve anything else. A big sack of fur was weighing me down.

"Visko!" I heard it squeak.

It was a familiar voice. I lifted my muzzle and saw a female dormouse. I said to myself, "What the hell's going on?" Not only was she absolutely gorgeous, but she was more like Ljuba than Ljuba herself. She was the quintessence of Ljuba.

"There are you, Viskovitz, the one who's always dreaming me," she said, chuckling.

I looked around, perplexed. What was Ljuba doing in reality? "Ljuba? What are you doing here?"

"I told you I wanted to do what you asked me to, but I prefer to do it here, not in that silly dream."

If this was a joke, it was truly in poor taste. I'd heard people say that reality is a dream, but I'd never believed it: who could be so perverse as to make a dream out of stuff like that?

"I don't know who sent you, Ljuba, but they've certainly made a mistake. Look, this is no place for you. Do you smell that stench? It's acid rain, nitrates, sulfur. Every square inch of this neighborhood is polluted. Here you have to wear yourself out to live. It's full of noise, disease. There are martens, owls, weasels. There's man. I have an extremely jealous mate and fourteen children. It's a cursed reality, Ljuba, you'll never be happy here, you'll never find peace . . ."

"That's not necessarily so . . ."

"Believe me, sweetness."

"Not anymore, Visko."

"Not anymore?"

She curled her tiny lips in an enigmatic sweet smile and squeaked out: "All this exists only because I have chosen to imagine it, Visko. This isn't 'life,' it's my hibernation. The reason you were always dreaming me is that I willed it. I didn't ever tell you because I wanted it to come as a surprise. It amused me to toy with you."

"That's good, that's really good. And I suppose you dreamed Jana, Zucotic and all the others?"

"Certainly. I made them such losers because I wanted you all to myself, dear. You don't believe it? Watch this."

Before my eyes I saw three acorns pop out of the ground—big as watermelons, without caps, without husks.

"Until today, Visko, I was too shy. It's not easy to go up to someone and say, 'You're the dormouse of my dreams.' I wanted you to look for me, I wanted you to dream me. I wanted to test you. Now I know that you love me, my treasure, I'm not afraid. I want to make you happy. We don't have any more time to lose, Visko, all dreams come to an end. Come."

She made a bed of chamomile blossoms appear, and she lay down on it.

"The reality is that I am even lazier and sleepier than you, Visko, and there is nothing I wish for more than to sleep in your arms, than to hear you snore in my sleep."

She opened her mouth in a yawn that was so brazenly open it seemed that her very soul would slip out . . .

Exulting, I melted away. I didn't fully understand who was dreaming whom, but under my fur, my heart dissolved in an ocean of blessedness. With one thankful blink of my eyelids, I blessed all that dreariness—that foul lake and that polluted forest, that suffocating air and that sterile earth. That whole desolate worn-out world: only a yawn away from bliss.

But Don't You Ever
Think of Sex, Viskovitz?

Sex? I didn't even know I had one. Imagine when they told me I had two of them.

"We snails, Visko," my old ones explained to me, "are insufficient hermaphrodites—"

"How disgusting!" I shrieked. "Even our family?"

"Certainly, sonny. We are able to fulfill both the masculine function as well as the feminine one. There's nothing to be ashamed of." With his radula, he pointed to my two tools.

"And how come insufficient?"

"Because we can couple only with other snails, if there is a reciprocal inclination, but never with ourselves."

"Says who?"

"Our faith, Visko. The other nasty thing is a mortal sin. Even to think of it," Daddymommy warned.

"And it is also impure conduct to shut yourself up in the shell, talk to yourself and be too pleased with yourself," added Mommydaddy.

A shudder of terror rippled my mantle.

"It's high time you started looking around for a good match; the reproductive season lasts only a few weeks."

Perplexed, I stretched out my tentacles in various directions. "But the nearest snails are months away!"

"You're mistaken, sonny, there are some excellent young ones in the neighborhood."

But nearby I could see just Zucotic, Petrovic and Lopez, my old schoolmates.

"You must be joking. You don't think that I—"

"They come from good families, with a pretty good genetic inheritance and good evolutionary prospects. Beauty isn't everything, Visko."

"But have you looked at them?" I pointed my rhinophor toward Zucotic, a gaunt gastropod with a shell that was practically clypeiform, an invaginated eye, an atrophied ctenidium. He revolted even predators. Did they really want to have grandchildren like this?

"With time you'll change your mind. You'll see. We snails have a saying: 'Love thy neighbor, because he who is far away will remain so.'"

"I'd rather be dead." I said goodbye and retreated inside

my shell. I carefully closed the operculum and sealed it with calcified salts, because one never knows.

"It's not done to lock yourself inside the shell, little Visko, people will think ill of it." The hell with people.

In the days that followed, for one reason or another, I was unable to think of anything but sex, or the sexes, that is.

It began as indefinable itches, little hormonal disturbances that made my gaze linger on the folds of some snails' mantles, trying to guess the shape under the shell, admiring the undulations of the foot. Nothing to be sick about, you understand, or to lose sleep over. Some of the snails in the garden were not bad, morphologically speaking, but snails who really suited my purpose, who had the class and the zoometric requisites to go with a Viskovitz, were nowhere to be found. I came to the conclusion, therefore, that they did not exist and that probably none had ever been born.

I was mistaken.

Her majesty the gastropodic beauty appeared suddenly among the heads of lettuce. He was rather distant, but I made out her breathtaking profile voluptuously spread out in the sun, the generous shapes barely contained by the trim shell.

Parbleu!

Bewitched, I stopped sleeping and eating. For my ocular antennae there suddenly was only she-he. I began to secrete mucus for no reason. But what could I do? My flame was at least two snail-years away! If I sprinted off then and there and started running like mad, even forgoing hibernation, I would still get there old and decrepit.

Unless . . . yes. I was thinking just that. What madness. What if she-he started running toward me? In that case, the point of contact would be among the squash blossoms, and we would unite as two middle-aged snails. The more I thought about it, the more I was seduced by the romantic grandeur of that gesture. I was consumed with yearning and anticipation. The sacrifice of youth for love's promise. And wasn't love always a great wager?

Was she-he looking? He-she was looking. Clearly, she-he had noticed me. It was very, very clear. You had to be bivalve not to get the signs of willingness that he-she was sending with his-her antennae.

"Viskoooo!" shouted Mommydaddy. "It's not good to talk to yourself. People will think ill of it."

"Let them think."

"Pull yourself together! Mr. Lopez is coming to visit."

Lopez was closing in frantically, drooling mucus and slipping in it, his face convulsed with lust, with dilated osfredia, a drooping mesenchyma, a flaccid radula, panting, and now only two days away from me. Moreover, a few more hours away, Petrovic and Zucotic were charging in my direction, set on a death race to have me, to pleasure themselves with my young body. I felt a chill in my hemolymph, and my palleale cavity stiffened. I extruded my esophagus in a spasm of horror.

I turned my eyes toward the lettuce and in an instant—
one of those instants in which a life is determined—the
choice was made.

"I'm coming!" I shouted.

And she-he also set him-herself in motion.

After six months of running I was a wreck.

Passionate impulses are not for mollusks, especially us
snails. I had rashes on my squamae, and my mesenchyma
was in pieces. With the end of the reproductive season,
the hormonal levels had dropped, and the romantic agita-
tions had dropped with them. Youth had vanished, and
my mucus was drying up.

I could see my body changing faster than the view. If
life is a race against time, well, one thing is certain, against
us snails time is the odds-on favorite.

At the start of my journey, I had deluded myself that,
worst-case scenario, I would have at least seen the world,
virgin territories and foreign cultures inches-upon-inches
away. But I was coming to see that the whole world was
vegetables. I had deluded myself that I could make a clean
break with the past, but every time I turned my antennae,
relatives and acquaintances were there, wearing disap-
proving and furious expressions, their stares loaded with
reproof. The snails of our childhood are forever in our
field of vision, as are those of our old age. Casual meetings don't exist for us, nor does privacy. It is clear, then,
why one needs a shell, despite the trouble of having to lug
it around on one's back.

But I kept running toward him-her, sighing and dreaming with eyes wide open, at night, under the moon, with the scent of parsley and the wind's caress on my squamae. And she-he also was coming toward me. That was all that mattered.

Winter came, and after three months, spring and the buds of the first squash blossoms.

And then, the long-awaited moment.

I was dismayed, the world had crumbled under my foot. No wonder he-she was coming toward me, was responding to my calls. She-he was my reflected image. I circled the spigot and saw myself quietly weeping my last drops of mucus. Poor Viskovitz. I felt for me an infinite tenderness. Then I leaned on that chromed surface and began to howl with laughter.

What else could I do? I was laughing. No. We were laughing. But my image immediately became serious and began to look at me attentively. How beautiful I was! So pliably feminine and vigorously virile. I couldn't tear my eyes away from myself: I was still a superb animal, probably the most attractive one who had ever existed, extraordinarily sexy for a mollusk. A sensual radula on squamae out of a fairy tale, an elastic and compact physique, a shell that was camouflaged but elegant, and reproductive equipment . . . *Parbleu!* In an instant the meaning of this event was clear to me. I timidly bent my ocular antennae toward each other, and for the first time my right pupil stared into my left one. I felt the short circuit, the shudder in my soul, and was able to stammer only one banal sentence:

"I love you, Viskovitz."

"Me too, silly."

With my radula I delicately caressed my pneumostome, with the distal part of my foot I brushed the proximal. I felt the warm pressure of the rhinophor slipping under my shell, and a strong agitation froze the center of my being. "Oh, heavens! What am I doing?" I stammered. But I gave myself up to my embrace, I clung to my flesh. Inebriated with desire, I pressed myself to me, I throbbed at the clammy touch of my epidermis, I drank of the viscous liquid of mucus, greedily straining to possess those adorable limbs. I clutched them desperately.

When I was done, I realized that in the frenzy I had come out of my shell and was lying on my back, with my sexes waving in the breeze. And that everyone's eyes were aimed at me. In a half-foot radius alone there were three families of snails, and you can imagine their reactions.

"How gross. What a thing to have to see!" a neighbor complained.

"You will be damned forever, Viskovitz," snapped another. They yelled at their children to turn the other way, but they themselves took care not to turn their antennae.

"We will teach you a lesson," they threatened. As if a

snail had ever beaten up another snail. I had taken enough abuse, so instead of retiring inside my shell, I stood up before them.

"Insufficient hermaphrodites yourseeeeelves!" I screamed at those hypocrites.

The days that followed were the happiest of my life. The spring breeze had brought the homage of two big yellow petals, and I languidly stretched myself on them and bathed myself in their scent, happy to be a mollusk and in love. I had taken this new abode in place of my shell, too unsuited to the complex geometry of hermaphrodite eroticism. But my story had not stopped causing scandal.

"This is nothing but a typical example of the collapse of gastropodic society," said one. "The 'I' has replaced society, and the narcissistic personality triumphs. We are falling back on the personal and the private."

I confess that I was falling back on my privates rather willingly. It was one of the few advantages of not having a spine.

And there were those who sought to psychoanalyze me: "When you have secondary narcissism, frustrated love turns on itself and gives birth to delusions of grandeur, to the overestimation of the self. The 'I' believes itself to be God."

No, it had never occurred to me that I was God. If anything, He was the one who started those rumors.

"The advancement of old age shatters the dream of the blessed extension of childhood's omnipotence, and the self-protective mechanism of narcissism breaks down . . ."

I had to admit that I hated growing old. Old age made me become jealous. More than once I had caught myself fantasizing about a younger snail, and my heart had broken to pieces. Naturally I was that snail, my youthful image spread out on the lettuce, but that didn't make the pain any less. During such moments I locked myself in my shell and wept. I wasn't loving myself back. My eyes weren't looking at each other anymore.

But life went on, there was no getting around it—I was pregnant. I lived in terror that the stories about the dangers of self-fertilization were true, and that I would bear monsters. Types with a turreted shell or with a bifid foot who would make me feel guilty for the rest of my days.

I was mistaken.

As soon as I saw the tiny shell of my newborn son, Viskovitz, I recognized it. Her majesty the gastropodic beauty. He was the perfect copy of her parent, more like a divinity than a mollusk. So tiny it looked like a snail seen from a distance, *that* snail seen from a distance. How beautiful she was! I delicately caressed his pneumostome, with the distal part of my foot I caressed her proximal . . .

"I love you, Viskovitz," he answered.

As in fairy tales, love triumphed. But this time there would be no end. There would never be an end.

"How gross! The things we have to see!" a neighbor complained.

You're Losing Your Head, Viskovitz

I asked my mother, "What was Daddy like?"

"Crunchy, a bit salty, rich in fiber."

"Before you ate him, I mean."

"He was a little guy, insecure, anxious, neurotic—pretty much like all you baby boys."

I felt closer than ever to the parent I had never known, who'd been dissolved in Mom's stomach just as I was being conceived. From whom I had gotten not nurturing but nourishment. I thought, Thank you, Dad. I know what it means for a mantis to sacrifice himself for the family.

I stood still for a moment of recollection before his tomb, that is to say my mother, and said a Miserere.

After a bit, since thinking about death never failed to give me an erection, I figured that the time had come to catch up with Ljuba, the insect I loved. I'd met her about a month earlier at my sister's wedding, which was also my brother-in-law's funeral. And I'd remained a prisoner of her cruel beauty. Since then we'd kept on seeing each other. How had that been possible? God had blessed me with the most precious gift he could give a mantis: premature ejaculation. A necessary condition for any love story that isn't ephemeral. The first week I'd lost a pair of legs, my pincers. The second week the prothorax with the connectors for flying. The third week . . .

My friends Zucotic, Petrovic and Lopez started yelling from the higher branches where they'd settled: "Don't do it, Visko, for the love of heaven!" For them, females were the devil, misogyny their mission. They had been sexually deviant or dysfunctional since metamorphosis. They had taken priestly vows, and they spent the whole blessed day chewing petals and reciting psalms. They were very religious.

But there wasn't a prayer that could stop me, not once I heard the icy sigh of my mistress, the hollow rustling of her membranes, her funereal, mocking laugh. I moved frenetically in the direction of those sounds with the one leg I had left, using my erection as a crutch, making every effort to visualize the glory of her curvaceous shape, which I couldn't see since I no longer had ocelli, which I couldn't smell since I no longer had antennae, which I couldn't kiss since I no longer had palpi.

By now I'd lost my head.

You're Getting a Little Cuckoo, Viskovitz

After a lot of migrating I found a neat little place in a beech grove in Upper Bavaria. An uncrowded, luxuriant territory with a nice view of the lake, but above all just two wing beats away from a grain field. That's the stuff—grain. I don't know about you, but I'm by preference granivorous. I can get along as a fructivore or insectivore, and I *can* eat snails and things like that. The truth is that we talented finches end up doing well in whatever ecosystem you put us in. I've toured lots of habitats, and you can take my word for it—there isn't a better place to nest than right here. It was time to get around to starting a family, time for my offspring to be born, wide-awake guys like their father, eager to put into practice the teachings of old Viskovitz. So, while it was still winter, before it was hormones telling me what to do, before anyone else got around to it, I set about building a nest. I had plenty of time to plan it, find the best materials, get it in tip-top shape. I happen to know that the nest is the first thing a she-finch looks at. When I'd finished it up, all the nubile females in the area—not all that many, to tell the truth—began to gather round.

I wasn't so much looking for showy plumage in the mother of my chicks as a healthy robust physique (while still feminine), a well-developed ovipositor, a vigilant sense of responsibility and an unshakable morality.

For this I chose Ljuba.

"Oh, Visko, it's a dream," she chirped when she'd barely put a claw on the veranda. She couldn't believe her eyes.

On the right, just past the entrance, there was the egg nook lined with down, with vents to regulate the air flow and temperature. On the left there was the breakfast nook with storage space for shelled grain and other supplies. The upper story was a sumptuous alcove with a view of the lake, waterproofed and lined with feathers, grasses, wool and flowers. The weight-bearing members of the structure rested solidly on a frame of beech twigs, after the fashion of weaver sparrows. It was held together with clay and saliva, the way swallows build, and it was finished off with dried dung. I had camouflaged the outer walls with sweet-smelling ivy, just enough to hide them from the eyes of predators but not so much that my neighbors wouldn't burst with envy. And in due course I would build another nest, the way some moorhens do—down by the lake with a sun deck.

"Oh, Visko, is it all yours?"

"*Ours,* my little chickadee."

"I'm so excited."

She was in the middle of her first ovulation. I made allowances for that. "That's love," I explained. "After a while it passes." I asked her to come upstairs.

"Oh, Visko . . ."

After a few days we were expecting our first chicks.

Waiting for the blessed event, I passed the time on the terrace admiring my territory. I thought it odd that there was so little competition around here—only three sparrows looking a bit befuddled. In time I'd be able to extend my territory all the way to the wheat fields. You really had to envy my future heirs. With a father like me, their life would be one long triumphal march.

I began to hop from branch to branch for no particular reason—because I felt like it, because they were *my* branches.

Suddenly I heard a suspicious noise, and I spied a feathered creature moving cautiously into my territory, getting close to my possessions.

I sang out, "Hold it right there, finch!"

"Sorry, Visko. It's me, Petrovic . . . I'm wounded."

My neighbor Petrovic was dragging himself along the ground, his feathers dripping with blood as if someone had hit him with birdshot. Who had cut him down like that?

"The cuckoo, Viskovitz. He did a number on me."

I admit that I didn't know much about the subject of cuckoos. I thought they only came out of clocks and went "cuckoo." Petrovic painted a far more disturbing picture. They were animals five times bigger than us . . . and they had a nasty habit.

"Reproductive parasitism?! What are you trying to say?"

"Those bastards have no morals, Visko. They don't build nests, they get it on when they feel like it—on branches, without any courtship or wedding. Then they leave their eggs in someone else's nest . . . chuck out one of yours and put in theirs. And then sometimes the little bastards kick your children out of the nest. It's a massacre. It happened to Lopez."

"Holy tempest!"

"And if you're so dense that you don't catch on, it ends up with you feeding him for months, thinking he's your child. That's what happened to Zucotic. He's been taking care of him for a year. He goes around with a cuckoo four times his size, saying, 'Look how big my boy is!' No one has the nerve to tell him the truth."

"Blessed birdseed!"

"This year I caught the cuckoo in the act—he was changing the eggs in my nest and I read him the riot act."

But apparently it had been the cuckoo who had the last word.

My thoughts flew immediately to Ljuba. She might be laying at any moment. I had to get to my nest in a hurry and stand guard. I said goodbye and took off.

"Never take your eyes off the clutch," Petrovic yelled after me. "It only takes an instant!"

I found Ljuba in the living room, sprawled on a cushion of flowers. She confirmed everything that Petrovic had said. "Everyone knows about cuckoos, they're a fact of life. But we don't have to worry, Visko. This nest is a bunker. And you're not as dumb as your neighbors."

"Right, right. But better safe than sorry."

I waited for three days without closing my eyes until the eggs were laid. God granted us three of them, white and perfectly oval. I measured them, and then with my beak I inscribed a "V" on each of them. Ljuba kept me from using dyes—what if they got through to the yolk?

We had to stay alert. We set up tours of duty for standing watch and for brooding. We had enough food so we wouldn't have to leave the nest. I kept watch behind the door; if someone stuck his beak in, I'd let him have it between the eyes. I couldn't stop thinking about that story about cuckoos, about how for centuries we passeriforms had been duped. I felt wounded in my dignity as a finch. The truth is that many of us *passeres,* including finches, have a bad habit of behaving in a stereotypical way. If we see a straw doll with a hat, we think it's a farmer. If we see a chick with its mouth open, it has to be fed. So of course folks take advantage of us. One of the first things I would teach my children: the virtue of doubt.

In the dead of night I put my ear against the shell and listened to the little darlings breathe.

When it was time for Ljuba to stand guard, I allowed myself a short nap. When I woke up I found her sprawled on a pile of down—snoring!

I made a scene. I called down the holiest feathered saints on her head.

"Calm down, Visko. Your 'V's are still right there. I just gave birth—you can't go on torturing me like this."

"You still have the nerve to open your beak! You think I've slaved all my life for the great pleasure of raising cuckoos? You think my kind have held on for millennia of genetic competition so one day a fucking cuckoo can have a baby-sitter?!"

I turned around to check the eggs, and I swear that one of those "V"s was in a strange beakwriting. I spent another three days without closing my eyes, pacing around the eggs, praying and cursing. My nerves on edge all the way to the tips of my feathers.

Then they finally hatched. Two boys and a girl. They made a certain impression: three little unfeathered bodies with huge gaping mouths going *cheep cheep.*

"Aren't they darling?"

"I suppose so," I answered warily. I stopped to examine the one in the middle. He was clearly different from the other two. "Look—this one has reddish down."

"He's just got a little yolk stuck to him, Visko. That's all."

"Okay, but it'd be a good idea to keep an eye on him. And why the hell is he squawking louder than the others?"

"Because you've been ruffling his feathers for an hour."

"Could be. But it'd be better to separate him from the other two."

"You're joking. Do you have any idea what a trauma that would be for the poor little thing? Be reasonable for a second—if he were what you're afraid of, he'd be the biggest of the three, but the other boy is bigger."

"Okay. It'd be a good idea to keep an eye on him, too."

When I said the word "eye," my own began to cross. How long a damned time had it been since I'd been able to close them?

"The little ones need protein, Visko. Get busy—hunt up an earthworm, a snail, a grass snake. Yes, best of all would be a nice little grass snake."

A grass snake? Easier said than done. Where could I find a grass snake at this time of night?

I took off anyway. What with the fresh air and smacking my head on branches, I half woke up. I flew all over the place. But once again my skill and minute knowledge of the territory paid off. At dawn I returned to the nest with a first-rate grass snake.

"Bravo, Visko," my Ljuba twittered. "I knew you could do it. Hand it over."

"Oh, no. I want to feed them the grass snake myself!"

I divided my prey into three parts. I shredded them and started feeding the little girl.

"Thanks, Papa," she chirped.

"Did you hear that? She already knows how to say 'papa'! She's certainly one of ours."

After that I fed the boy with the yellow down.

"Thanks, Papa," he mumbled.

"Did you hear him? This one's got his act together."

Then I took the last piece and gave it to the one with the reddish down.

"Thanks, Visko," he rasped. "The grass snake's not bad."

I felt a cold shudder in my bones.

"It's him!" I cried to heaven. "It's him! I knew it was him, the bastard!" I grabbed him by the scruff of the neck. "Admit it! Admit it, you miserable son of a bitch! You wanted to screw me over, eh? You thought you could get away with it, you deformity?"

The guy started crying as if I'd slit his throat. Ljuba jumped on me and started raising hell. I ended up with my wings pinned to the floor.

"Don't you dare touch my babies or I'll kill you!" she erupted. "As God is my witness, if I hear one more word about cuckoos, I'm taking my little ones and clearing out!" She was furious. "On second thought, I'm leaving now!"

"Wait, sweetness. Let's not be hasty. You know I love you and the babies, you're everything to me. Forgive me, I don't know what I'm doing. This story about cuckoos—"

"I don't want to hear that word again!"

"Okay, okay. Maybe all I need is a good rest. A good long rest." The little one kept on yowling in Ljuba's wings. I couldn't take it anymore. "I'll take a nap, Ljuba. Don't forget—keep an eye on them . . . I mean . . . you take care of everything." I dropped like a stone.

When I woke up, Ljuba and the kids had disappeared. The nest was torn apart, as if a hawk had been through it.

"Ljuba!" I shouted.

"We're here on the veranda, Visko. It's time to get more food, dear. The grain is all gone."

"All gone! Damn! How long did I sleep?"

"Three days, dear."

The kids were basking in the sun. I observed them carefully. "Anyone acting strange, Ljuba?"

"Only you, Viskovitz."

They'd already grown a promising set of feathers. Ash gray on the cheeks, throat and breast, dull black with white spots on the pinions and tail feathers. They looked okay, as alike as three drops of water. Very good. It was time to celebrate. I still had some currants in the attic, and I went to get them. As I got to the top floor, my eyes played a nasty trick on me. My feathers stood on end, and I froze on the spot with my beak gaping. Somebody was in my bunk. A great big bird was lolling on my feather bed!

"Ljuba!" I yelled. "What's going on?!"

Ljuba rushed upstairs. Meanwhile, that guy on the bed jumped to his feet. He was as big as Ljuba—four times bigger than me. His breast feathers were ash gray and his pinions were dull black with white spots. He opened his beak and said, "Cuckoo, Viskovitz."

I saw my little ones coming upstairs. Not all that little—they were already taller than me by a beak.

"Cuckoo, Viskovitz," they chorused.

Then I looked at Ljuba and saw her smile.

"Cuckoo, Viskovitz," she chimed in.

My head was spinning. I didn't know what to say.

"Cuckoo," I answered politely.

You've Got Horns,
Viskovitz

I, Viskovitz, am good and kind, but when I lower my antlers . . .

I let out a bellow and charged.

That's the way it's always been among us elks: whoever wins gets all the girls in heat for himself. The other bull-elks are crushed; all that's left is fantasies. Right now there was only one adversary left between me and glory, love and power. I could not fail, I couldn't let one instant of distraction or trivial fear ruin a year of athletic preparation and ground-pawing anticipation . . .

I came down on him with the speed of a warhorse,

with the whole half-ton of my weight. But just as I made my thrust, Petrovic, my rival, played dirty. He tucked himself up like a rat and flipped me into the air. He hit me on a leg joint and I collapsed. I ended up with my snout in the ground and all I could do was ask for mercy. Petrovic gave me another swipe with his antlers and then went off in the direction of the cow-elks to get his reward.

That evening I limped off into the undergrowth to lick my wounds in private. Then I dragged myself as far as the watering hole and looked for Jana.

"Hi, Jana," I croaked.

"You smell awful, Viskovitz." The darkness of the evening mercifully covered her. As she grazed, her teats hung down, brushing the ground. "They made a real mess of you this time, Visko," she sneered.

If you picked off her lice, she would always go for a stroll with you, and if you scratched her scabies sores, she would even bray out something like "You're the best, you're the champion, you're number one."

That's how we spent our winter.

Meanwhile, you got in training for spring. And you sharpened your antlers. Because you're an elk, and up there coming out of your head you don't just have thoughts—you have sabers.

When the new season came and the females were in heat again, there we bachelors were at the foot of the mountain, deciding who would face Petrovic. To my strength, a natural gift, I'd added a good bit of experience—all those tricks you learn with time. It only took me a quarter of an hour to make Lopez and Zucotic and others understand that I was still the number-one contender. A few of the younger ones had mistaken my circumspection for fear, and they were now in the bushes licking their wounds. Petrovic, who had been following all this from the mountaintop, charged immediately. This time I was waiting for him at the end of the valley, hooves planted. I saw that he was aged and run-down, thin and unsteady. I slammed him into an oak tree a couple of times until I felt sorry for him.

Having settled that business, I set off up the mountain where the cow-elks were waiting for me. Their little heads were peeping out from behind the boulders. In the air I caught the scent of females and heard some sweet murmurings.

"Who won?"

"Viskovitz. He's on his way up."

When I got right in front of them, they didn't exactly fit what comes to mind when you think of a herd of females in heat. You imagine them all atwitter, shivering and whinnying. A couple of them were snoring. Others were stretched out on their bellies, swishing their tails across their backs. Some were browsing. However, the most appetizing of the bunch came forward and whinnied, "I am the prime female of the group. You, having won the fight, are the pride of the herd, our lord and master, and you will couple with me first and then with all the others, and we will give birth to your vigorous and abundant offspring."

"You can count on it," I grunted.

"Naturally you will have to see to the security and prosperity of the herd. You will discover and conquer new territories, and you will always watch over our feeding grounds. You will keep the wolf and the lynx away, and you will stand guard night and day on the mountaintop to catch the scent of hunters. You will be feared by other herds and you will defend our territory.

"Since you are the only one with antlers, you will pull down the higher branches so that we can browse, and you will pick the parasites out of our coats. You will be an example for your sons, and you will see to their education. When we are pregnant you will satisfy our least whim. You will settle every fight, always governing wisely and judging fairly. You will not associate with the other males on the mountain, and you will keep us away from their impure seed. During the mating season you will face rivals in the arena until one day, when you are old and tired, you will succumb to challengers who are younger and fresher, among whom you may find your own sons. And you will be killed. Your antlers will join those of your predecessors, to whom we have never lessened our grateful and reverent homage. My name is Ljuba."

"And I'm Viskovitz, my treasure," I nickered. "You have a beautiful coat, Ljuba. You know what I'd like to do now, my little blossom? You and I are going to take a little stroll into the bushes . . ."

"I'm afraid that's not possible. When you wish to couple with me—I gather that's what you're driving at—you must do it here, on the mountainside. The herd must not be left unguarded."

"Here? In front of everyone?"

"That is the rule, Your Elkness."

"Okay, we'll talk about this later, when it gets dark. But, my filly, do me a favor—call me Visko."

That evening, after sunset, I was on sentry duty. The night was peaceful. The little ones were sleeping curled up between the legs of my cow-elks, who were snoring. Only Ljuba continued to graze. Every so often she gave me a look. I whistled and she broke into a trot. It was clear that we understood each other right away. The moon made her dewy eyes glisten. I began to fondle her. I felt a certain tormented urgency. Hey—it's more than understandable. I hoisted myself onto her rump. I held her steady with my forelegs, I nipped her neck with my teeth. With my—

"What was that noise?"

"I'm afraid that a wolf has seized one of the little ones, Your Grace."

"Well, as long as it's not one of mine. It'll be one less to—I mean—of course I'll get right down and take care of it . . . But I beg you, call me Visko."

A slobbering wolf had seized an elk-calf by the throat and was slinking off to pluck it apart in the forest. I butted him in the rear and sent him flying. But just then another pair of those lousy bastards popped out of the woods, and now I had one of them hanging on my hock. I shifted my weight onto my forelegs and gave a kick to get him off. They'd picked the wrong day. I ran the third one through with a heavy thrust, and that finished him off. The others broke away, and I could tell I wouldn't see them again for a good while. But by then the evening was ruined. I was bleeding from two legs and my stomach. It'd been a long day. I lowered myself onto my back, belly in the air, and let the mares lick my wounds. I heard one of them say to another, "What did I tell you? I knew Visko would straighten them out." Then I collapsed.

The following day, before I'd recovered, the lynxes showed up, and then toward evening a couple of elk bastards came up from the valley, attracted by the scent of the girls. It wouldn't have been hard to take care of these guys if not for the shape I was in. I was a dishrag. But you can imagine what would've happened if I let these guys have their way. I decided to gamble. I forced myself into a trot, pretending my legs were in working order. Only God knows that I was cursing with pain. Then, facing the more combative of the two, I let out what we call "the ultimate bellow," the one that up here, just like down on the plain, means a fight to the finish. My luck held. They headed off. But if they'd had the guts to charge . . . it's better not to think about it. I heard the girls say, "He's got what it takes, that Visko. Did you see? Those other guys pissed on themselves." Then I tumbled to the ground.

The next day I began to feel better. I got my strength

back and with it a certain languorous yearning. I decided to dedicate the day to Ljuba. I called to her and she didn't make me ask twice. But I noticed right away that she was a little nervous.

"Are you still afraid of your good old Visko?" I snorted with a horsey little smile.

"It's not that, my lord. It's that I heard a shot. It came from the woods."

"You must have imagined it, dear. Calamities can't all come at once. It's just a little emotion—I myself . . ."

I heard a crack, then a strangled mooing in the forest.

"I'll see what I can do. But do me a favor—next time call me Visko."

I went down into the woods and attracted the attention of the hunters while the herd got away to safety. I bounded off, going this way and that, over hill and dale, leaving tracks and erasing tracks. I took two slugs and a hail of buckshot. Then, in the dead of night, I dragged myself back to the mountaintop.

A pair of she-elks were still awake. I heard one bray to the other, "What a guy, that Viskovitz! With him around we can sleep in peace." Then I collapsed.

The next day I woke up in a great mood. In our neck of the woods, hunters don't show up more than once a week. I'd taught the wolves and lynxes a good lesson, and as for the bull-elks . . . they'd better steer clear. It was a mild sunny day, and when the air is clear, the spectacle of the Rocky Mountains is something to see. Maybe it's because I'm an elk, but to me those sharp peaks look like invincible antlers. I bugled. Because I felt like it. I would have liked it if, from the other mountains, some herd bosses had answered. Because we elks are here on all these peaks. The little brats were grazing happily. The herd was peaceful. I had a bite of grass and then I called the girls over. How nicely the little fillies trotted! We had some unfinished business to take care of. There was no reason to wait for evening—from now until then I would take my pleasure. There was really no need for modesty in my own home. There was Ljuba, then there was Lara, then there was Elke, then there was Olga . . . Great Elk, I felt as excited as a young buck!

"Girls, today we're all going to work together to make sure our herd has an abundant and vigorous offspring," I neighed. "Step right up, Ljuba."

"I'm afraid that's not possible, my lord."

"Don't say that, not even as a joke . . ."

"The mating season is over, my lord, and we'll have to wait until next year for these things, if we'll still have the honor of having you with us. In the meantime, you remain our only master. If you would be so kind as to pull down that branch, we . . ."

Jana was lying in a pond, half submerged in the slime that covered her scabs.

"Your Elkness," she brayed, "you smell awful."

ALL THAT GLITTERS IS NOT GOLD, VISKOVITZ

As soon as I was born, I got compliments.

"How beautiful he is," Mama crowed. "He's already a perfect beetle. He has more color than the others, he's more attractive!"

She was completely happy with what she saw. Brand-new, I must have been a pretty sight.

I congratulated myself on coming into the world and took a look around to make sure there were no predators. I would have been annoyed if the party ended so soon. Around me there was a bunch of snot-noses who had barely completed their larval stage. They were trying to get out of their "pears," making an effort to move around. I liked the idea that I was starting life with an advantage over them, even if it was as ephemeral as beauty. But Papa managed to dampen my enthusiasm.

"Don't listen to your mother, Visko. Beauty is no advantage at all for creatures like us."

"Is that right?"

"I'm sure of it, son. And it would be good for you to know right off how things stand. We're dung beetles, kid, and the only thing that matters in our life is . . . well, look . . . it's shit."

I was stunned. I wasn't able to take in what he meant, but the way he said it, hunching up in his shell with a mortified expression, weighed on me uneasily.

"But we should have a party now," he continued. "This is a delicacy, you'll like it." With a certain apprehension he held out a little dark ball with his appendages. I warily tasted it, just a little lick. It was disgusting. My God, I thought, do our lives really depend on this filth?

"You are our first son, Visko. It wasn't easy to bring you into the world. To grow a larva it takes a ball of material two inches thick. We call them 'pears,' and they don't grow on trees."

"There's a lot of competition?"

"You said it, kid. There's a drought and there aren't big herds, so the vital matter is scarce, and there are a lot of us. When a two-pound load drops, in the span of ten minutes you'll find something like five thousand dung beetles—as well as endocopridi, scavatori and rotoletori . . ."

"Endocopridi?"

"Yes, they're scarabs, too, tiny little bastards who sneak into the balls you're rolling, and they eat them from the inside out. They can even do it in the larva if you're not paying attention. Then there are heliocopris—they're diggers, real bulldozers, great big beasts who weigh almost an ounce.

"If you run into one of them, I'm telling you, son, you'd better do what he says."

"I'll remember, Papa."

"But most of all, you've got to keep an eye out for your own kind. Because digging up, rolling and pushing a pear is backbreaking work. It takes thirty minutes, twenty if you're in really good shape. Dung isn't all the same. When you make your pear test the moisture content and the consistency. Then you have to find any knobs, pull them off, make it round. Then you have to roll it—you have to prop it up with your head and shove it with your hind legs, and at the same time you have to use your claws like rakes, smearing all the feces you find onto it. These are operations that cost energy. And energy costs shit. So the most efficient strategy for getting a ball is to steal it. When you're all tired out and the pear is ready, you have to defend it as you would your life, or they'll carry it off by force. Even your best friends, the ones you grew up with. The material is more powerful than we are, Visko. It eats up your soul."

"Papa, what are these appendages under the elytra?" I threw it out to change the subject.

"They're membranous wings. They allow us to fly."

"Fly! Wow! That's great news!"

"Pay attention now—flying takes a heap of energy. First you've got to speed up your metabolism, increase your body temperature. To do that you have to shiver."

"Shiver?"

"Yes, shivering charges you with energy, gets you ready for action. But you have to have ingested enough material to be able to do it. These days your energy is barely enough for gathering your material, and the material is barely enough to give you energy. You can allow yourself to fly only to get to the manure in a hurry. In the end it always comes back to that, Visko."

"To the material?"

"Right. But don't think that what we do is contemptible or worthless. Just the other way around. We dung beetles are fundamental to the ecosystem. Not only do we remove the manure that otherwise would pile up on the ground and suffocate the plants, but we also aerate and fertilize the soil, as well as hold back the proliferation of parasites and pathogenic agents, not to mention reducing the number of flies that proliferate in the excretions." My father proclaimed this with as big a sense of pride as his metabolism would allow.

The next day we were up in the air early to make up for the time lost with my birth. I was beginning to feel guilty until at last we caught sight of a herd of elephants at a watering hole. Papa advised me to choose a specialization, and coprophagy of elephant products seemed the most promising. Even though it had been emphasized to me that these animals rarely stepped on their products, it was still hard to imagine that anyone would have the courage to go into the midst of them and carry away that stuff. And yet the first load was barely released when thousands of beetles materialized as if by magic and hurled themselves onto it. My father was among the first. I was to learn, to study his moves, to familiarize myself with the unexpected, but pretty soon the scene had turned into a dark hell of bodies and shit, an unintelligible chaos of hitting, yelling and swearing. I stood there, petrified, overcome by the stench, by the trumpeting of the elephants, by terror. I prayed to God to have pity on us.

It seemed to me a miracle when I saw the antennae of my father emerge from the melee. He was dragging himself along, clutching a good-sized piece of a ball—bigger than him—not so large as to give me a brother but enough calories to allow him to make it to his next battle. He signaled to me with his elytra. He was shaken up and bruised, but his buccal appendages were grinning with happy anticipation. His joy was short-lived, however, because two bad guys came out from under a leaf and began to pound on him. They turned him upside down and took the pear. My father got up and charged. They beat him up again. I ran to help him, but I still hadn't quite gotten the hang of shivering to accelerate my metabolism. So I ended up with my belly in the air, beaten. When I came to, I saw that all that was left of my father were a few scattered fragments. In the distance I could see his persecutors making off with the loot. With them was my mother, who hadn't taken long to jump on their bandwagon.

From that day on, shivering wasn't a problem. I was one against all. In that godless world, only one value survived: the Substance. In It I put my faith. I began to measure the meaning of life in grams.

I gathered a band of young toughs who raided and beat up the young and the old. I took part in all kinds of crime. I told myself that I wasn't the one who invented the law of the strongest. But two pears stolen from a family bug couldn't begin to satisfy my unlimited desire to own. So I decided to look for wealth at the very point of origin. I fastened myself onto the coat of the producing animals and let them carry me. That way I saved energy, and when they dumped a load I was always the first one there. If the wind carried the scent over a dead zone—a pond, for example—it could take as much as a half hour for the crowd to show up. It was hard work but well paid, and soon I had enough capital to set myself up on my own. I hired a staff and surrounded myself with a private militia. In a little while I found myself at the head of an organization that controlled acres of the savanna and had exclusive contracts with many herds. Moreover, we controlled the currency exchange, the futures markets and the fluctuation of savings rates. In the course of one season I had amassed a patrimony that was calculated in tons of substance, a good part of it in liquid assets.

I became the preeminent insect, the one to be admired and envied, the one who received a respect and adulation equal to that paid only to the thing itself. I thought that was all the happiness a beetle could hope for. But I was forced to change my mind.

I saw her on the corolla of an orchid. Her exoskeleton was red as the dawn, her corslet a whirlwind of golden reflections, a little sun caught among the petals. How to describe her? Her beauty was simultaneously adelphagous and polyphagous. Every part of her body, emimeron or episternum, prothorax, mesothorax or metathorax, ureters, stigma or scutellum was for my ocelli both joy and torment. She was the queen of scarabaeids, and I couldn't live without her. At last love had a face and a name: Ljuba.

I thought of delivering a bouquet of the precious currency, but it dawned on me that it was contraindicated. It wasn't with riches that I wished to storm the castle of her heart. She had just arrived with the monsoons and knew nothing about me. She liked talking about flowers, trees, resins, fruits, an unusual tendency in a beetle. She could chatter for hours without ever mentioning the brown substance. Ah, how refreshing it was to be with her! She was fascinated by everything that was sweet, perfumed, colored, and this passion of hers was so contagious that for the first time my life seemed an adventure full of wonder and mystery and the world a perfect place in which to celebrate the harmony between insects and creation.

I told her I loved her.

"And I like you, Visko. I'd like to be your mate."

"Do you mean you like me as I am, as an insect? That you have no interest in knowing how much I own?"

"Of course, what importance does that have?"

I felt myself melt. Was this real or a dream? Even beetles had hearts? We made the preparations for our nuptial flight and never—I say never—did she ask me for a present or even simply to be fed. At last, fully convinced of her sincerity, I decided to bestow on her the prize she deserved, and I took her to one of my properties, a bath of manure ten yards square, surrounded by my militia.

"It's all mine," I announced. "And this is only one of my holdings—an empire that reaches from here to Lake Victoria."

"You're joking."

"Not in the least. Look." I plunged in headfirst. "Come on! It's yours now, too!"

Ljuba couldn't believe her ocelli. "You're asking me to go in . . . to go into that?" she stammered.

"Absolutely. I understand your modesty, dear, but after all, we're dung beetles."

"If this is a joke, it's in truly bad taste, Visko. I am a

purebred malolontha, a May beetle! No one has ever called me a dung beetle."

"May beetle? I don't understand the difference."

"I see that you don't. Dung beetles are crude creatures with dark carapaces who eat unmentionable filth. We May beetles, on the other hand, have dazzling colors and feed on pollen, aromatic resins and other sweet things. We can fly for hours, and we love poetry, the dance, good company and, above all, cleanliness, Visko. I can assure you that until today I have never seen a great big May beetle like you soaking in shit. Now I have to go away because this place stinks and you disgust me."

She had shivered enough to fly across the ocean. I would probably never see her again.

There I was with my palps open, trying to make sense of it. Me, a May beetle? And Papa and Mama? So that was why they didn't look like me. My real parents must have forgotten where they left my egg. Maybe Papa and Mama were tired of being alone. My God! Was it possible that . . . I was completely confused. Who was I? What was I doing soaking in this stuff? I should pull myself out of it, go after Ljuba, explain my situation and build a clean life with her. I said to myself, "Come on, Visko, do it!" But I wasn't able to feel enough disgust to shudder, and without shuddering I couldn't charge my metabolism enough to fly. There was too much pleasure in that odiferous bath, the fragrance of that bog, in the satisfaction of seeing the rabble—not only Coleoptera but also Trichoptera,

Thysanoptera and Aphaniptera—pressing up against the barricade to look at me and dream. For an instant I thought I caught a glimpse of the integument of my old father and saw him tremble. Trembling with pride that his son had made it, that he was in it, in it up to his neck.

What a Pig You Are, Viskovitz

Pigs are born pigs, and we Viskovitzes have been pigs for millions of years. But it wasn't always easy to keep this in mind. We were in a village of Hmong nomads in southern China, where everyone lived under one roof—men, women and pigs. It isn't for nothing that the ideogram *jia* (a pig under a roof) means "family." We were so prized by these people that if there wasn't an available sow, it was the women who suckled the piglets.

This created a certain confusion in the minds of us pigs.

It was to make sure everything was crystal clear that my mother's last words before she was butchered were

"Always remember what you are, son—a pig. Always eat pig slop, behave and think swinishly. Make sure you live in a pigsty and wallow like that great hog, your father."

"Yes, Mama, I promise," I grunted as I sobbed. And then I stuck my snout in the trough so I wouldn't hear the noise of her being slaughtered.

The loss of my mother (blessings on that sow!) left an overwhelming void in me and marked, alas, the beginning of that lamentable chain of events which led to my ruin.

The celebration of the *chun jie,* the Chinese New Year, had begun. The Year of the Dragon gave way to the Year of the Snake. These were festive days for humans, mournful days for pigs. But there were still some happy occasions for us, opportunities for socializing and revelry. The inhabitants of the neighboring villages gathered for the New Year's dances, for the rites of planting and trade, and it was then that courtships took place and marriages were arranged. And we pigs were necessary for the wedding feasts.

And indeed a young woman from our hut was getting married to a boy from the next village, and this fellow presented himself with a marriage portion of two suckling pigs and a sow. It may not seem like much of a gift—but only to someone who didn't see the sow. She was the only thing I looked at during the whole ceremony. She was a Venus with plenty of lard and ham, with clear pig skin and a prognathous snout. An extra little whiff of babirusa (that wild pig of the Indies) and a little curled tail spoke sweetly to the most piggish parts of my heart.

She came forward, swaying with dignity. I saw right away that she considered herself the queen of porkers.

"I am Lju-ba," she oinked, "which in our dialect means 'pearl before swine.'"

Mother in heaven, what a dame!

"And I am Viskovitz," I grunted.

"Which means?"

"Nothing. That I'm a filthy pig named Viskovitz, madam. Come here . . . Do you know you have a really beautiful snout?"

"Snout? You mean to say . . . a beautiful appearance."

"Right, right." Grunting and drooling I grabbed hold of her back. "Oh, what beautiful hams—I mean *limbs,* Countess."

She spun around and whacked my head with a tusk so hard that I saw all ten *tien gan* of the lunar year.

"Who do you take me for? One of your pig sluts?"

"Hey. I don't see any other males in this pigpen."

"I belong to no one. Only to my own spirit, *lu wu,* which has been nourished by the teachings of the Eight Immortals, *Ba Xian,* and of the Five Hundred Saints, *Luo Han,* and by my mind, *fu,* which I have cultivated by the practice of the *Qui Gong* in accordance with the Five Canons, *Wu Jing,* and by my worthiness, *kun,* and by my life, *lin,* which is in the service of goodness and the Greater Swineness."

I was rendered speechless, salt pork. What do you say to a sow who talks to you about Swineness?!

She pointed at the humans with her hoof, at the bride and groom who were dancing. "Look at how considerately men treat their women. Am I any less than they?"

"Certainly not."

"I have gone through the ceremony of grooming, *shan tou,* I have gone through the casting of my auspicious horoscope, *ba zi,* but on this day of my *jie hun,* I would like to dance at least one dance."

I looked at the dancers. The rhythm didn't seem all that difficult, a rather monotonous 4/4.

"I'd give anything to dance with them, Viskovitz. Anything . . ."

And so it was, Mom, that even though I was driven by the most swinish intentions, I committed the first big mistake of my life. In dance time I strutted toward the scene of my damnation. Ljuba and I made a way for ourselves through the dancers, to the consternation of pigs and non-pigs alike. Balancing on our hind legs, we swayed, letting ourselves be carried away by the swing of the music. Intoxicated by the sound and by the opium fumes, I was moved to improvise more daring steps. Soon Ljuba and I were stealing the show. We were being applauded. We did spins, step-ball-changes, pirouettes, then twirled back into dancing cheek to cheek. When I realized how ridiculous I was, it was much too late. At these gatherings there were always dealers in jade and opium who were eager to acquire anything that could turn a profit. One of them saw how he could make money out of us.

We were sold to a circus in Shanghai. And so began the long *via crucis* of my mortification. My love for Ljuba became the theme for a clown act. It grew into a whole supershow performed by twelve pigs. There was a pig-tamer act, pigs on the flying trapeze and on bicycles. But above all there was the big dance finale with a dazzling dance number of pigs in white tutus, at the end of which I in a blue leotard and Ljuba in a pink tutu danced to a Strauss sonata.

All of us males were castrated.

At that point, Mom, it was hard for me to feel like a real swine. I tried desperately to wallow in mud, to grunt the most swinish obscenities, but it just wasn't the same. Every evening when I embraced Ljuba under the spotlights, I wasn't looking so much for the touch of skin on skin as for the communion of our souls. But in her eyes I saw only loathing for a fat castrated clown. And then the public applauded my tears and the solemn tragic essence of my rhythmic movement. The moment when I bowed to accept the tribute of the audience became more and more important to me. But as I was celebrating these new vain pleasures, I was also celebrating the totality of my downfall.

But my humiliation wasn't complete. One day, while we were touring Japan, an elderly Texas businesswoman came to my dressing room. She congratulated me and took the liberty of petting me. She went even further by buying me, paying, as I learned later, one hundred and twenty thousand dollars. I believe this figure is the highest that has ever been paid for a pig.

I flew with her to Dallas and from there in a private helicopter to her country house near Amarillo. The free and easy behavior of the old woman had at first led me to believe that she wanted to satisfy some extravagant erotic fancy. But it wasn't that. Nor was it that my owner was a member of some association for the benefit of pigs in general. No. The old woman had a sister who had recently kicked the bucket, leaving a will that said more or less this: "I bequeath all my worldly goods to that swine Adrian J. Stinson, the only guy who ever amused me and who could dance a fox-trot so that it felt like a tango."

Since poor old Mr. Stinson had already died in an old-age home, the old lady's lawyers arranged things so "that swine Adrian J. Stinson" ended up meaning me. I was the sole heir, so the money went into the pockets of the old lady. It was a dirty trick, a truly piggish thing to do. So I went along with the charade wholeheartedly. It wasn't hard for me to assume the role of "that swine," even if it wasn't altogether easy to dance a paso doble to the tune of that mazurka. The lawyers' skill and the power of the old lady did the rest. ("Lawyers these days can turn a case any which way they want, piggy.")

So that is how I found myself swimming in money, one of the largest fortunes in America. At that point there were no longer any limits to my degradation. I took to drowning my sorrows in champagne, chewing on Cuban cigars and hanging out with vacuous movie starlets and corrupt politicians. Until one day, during a reception in my honor, as I was staring at a plate of rolled ham slices, I decided to end it all. I tried to hang myself from a chandelier with my tie—ineffectively. Then I found a way to get to a window and jump out. But as luck would have it I bounced off an awning and landed on a pile of watermelons. I broke my bones but didn't put an end to my woes. The incident only increased my popularity, and here I am now going from network to network, launching a new line of merchandise, posing for magazine covers. The old lady says I'll be the first animal to become president of the United States, and as a matter of fact there's plenty of money for the campaign . . . What suffering, Mom. And you warned me.

The worst thing is that right now—when, thanks to my power, I can see the possibility of doing something for the good of swinehood and swinish values—I feel an increasingly perverse attraction for—an outright dependence on—symphonic music, Flemish painting, white flannels, French cheese, old silent movies, Rolls-Royces . . .

But I promise you, Mom, I promise you that if I am elected . . .

You've Made Progress, Viskovitz

I knew I was a genius even before I came into the world.

In the darkness of the womb, when my brothers were still shapeless embryos, excrescences on the placenta, I'd already found the way to the exit and started out a few weeks ahead of time. I knew I was destined to have an exceptional life, and I didn't want to waste any of it.

"You, Visko," my father announced, "are probably the most intelligent rodent who ever lived. They have worked in the laboratory for decades, using a process of artificial selection, to create a phenomenon like you. And your very name, V-I-S-K-O-V-I-T-Z, is an acronym for Very

Intelligent Superior Kind of Very Intelligent and Talented Zootype. Take pride in it."

"I am reasonably proud of it, Papa." Even before I was weaned I'd already figured out that by using acids or coagulative action I could derive rennet from my mother's milk and thus several varieties of aged cheese: both soft and string, and Taleggio, crescenza and provolone. In those days I'd also begun to exercise my musical talent on the wires of my cage and to pursue an interesting line of research in harmonic progressions, as well as the modal variations most in tune with the screams of pain emitted by the rats in the other sections. I succeeded in resolving their dissonances with felicitous counterpoint into a decently euphonious mode.

When they tried to measure my mental capacity, they soon realized that it was an impossible task. In the maze I never went down a blind alley. And as for their other crude aptitude tests, I knew the solutions before they even formulated the problems. How on earth could they measure me?

In those trials the lowest score, which defined the unit of stupidity, had been obtained by Zucotic, an extraordinarily obtuse subject produced by repeated inbreeding of the most imbecilic progeny of the laboratory. Ironically, that cretin's cage was next to mine, and the researchers seemed to give him the same kind of attention they gave to me, as if stupidity were a virtue comparable to genius. The oddity didn't end there. When we were assigned the

63

mates most genetically qualified to couple with us, it was immediately clear that in she-rats intelligence and beauty weren't coded into the same genes. My partner, Jana, was a graceless mole-brained alloglot, whereas Zucotic's partner, Ljuba—from her rodentian incisors to the last scales on her tail—was the most perfect form that the most imaginative mind (mine, that is) could conceive. So, while I was stuck listening to Jana dither disquisitively on the subject of ratiocination (she thought it meant reasoning like a rat), just one of her capacious incapacities, in the next cage beauty was being served up to idiocy.

Nor did I enjoy any greater recognition from the other lab rats. In our community, intelligence and culture were failings, not virtues. These wretches had suffered firsthand the brutality of the experimental method, and they had no faith in the promises of science or of reason in general. They dreamed of reaching the Sewer, the mythic place announced by a self-styled prophet who had emerged from a toilet bowl. A Shangri-la far from the villainies of civilization and progress. It was blessed with darkness and rot in which everything dissolved into a putrilaginous aromatic broth.

Given this state of affairs, the lab rats didn't put much faith in the usefulness of genius. But I knew with certainty that my intellect had been conceived for a purpose, that it was part of a transcendental power, call it what you will: history, the collective unconscious of topiform rodents, Divine Will . . .

It was a question of patience; my time would come.
And so it did.

One day Petrovic, a gigantic super-rat produced by genetic engineering, overpowered the mesh of his cage and, turning the handles from the outside, also freed the rats of Surgery, Pharmacy and Anatomy. A shapeless multitude of tortured and deformed wretches began to swarm across the tiles. No one—*ab invidia*—felt like liberating us privileged ones in the psychology department. It was only later, when it became clear that not one of those incapables had the slightest idea how to find the way to the sewer system or any other form of redemption, that it dawned on them: they had to turn to me.

"All-knowing V-I-S-K-O-V-I-T-Z, lord of the labyrinths, guide us," they implored me with unctuous flattery.

The laboratory corridors were arranged like a maze, so it was clear that I was the chosen rat, anointed to lead the exodus. What other purpose could there be for all those months of unraveling intricate puzzles, running through dark passageways, solving abstruse problems? Could I in good conscience turn away from my responsibility and refuse to guide my people?

"Forward march!" I squeaked and set off. I confidently started down the first corridor on the left and the second on the right.

During my experience with mazes, I had noticed that the most frequent solution to every problem of orientation was to take the first left and the second right. It wasn't necessary to be a genius to grasp that this would continue to be the solution.

And so it was.

After those two turns we found ourselves in the latrine. As soon as I realized that above us was a lever very like the ones I used to press down during my aptitude tests, everything became clear. I gave this lever a push, and the waters parted miraculously before my people. Every rodent was sucked toward our destination. A few minutes later we were splashing in the manna of the prophecy.

My companions looked around in amazement, overcome by the allure of this landscape. After years of sterile surroundings and medicinal doses, they were delighted by this impure and contaminated Nature, by this miasmic pool, by these moldy forests, by all this ordure. Parting the effluvia, I officially took possession of this territory in the name of my people. I gave a short celebratory speech and, using simple words suitable for this audience, sought to explain the juridical foundation on which I meant to build our society of rats. Without ever mentioning the term "eugenics," I nevertheless tried to make them see how advisable it would be for the future good of our people for me to have a "liaison" with all the super-she-rats present and to beget a super progeny worthy of representing our people.

But my words were suddenly interrupted by an attack of indigenous rats that sowed panic and confusion in our ranks. The bravest of us put up an honorable resistance, but soon the defeat was total.

Rat that I am, I slunk away.

It was soon clear that this place, far from being the promised land, was instead overrun by a barbaric horde of enraged vermin, even bigger than our super-rats and who, without any regard for Justice or Beauty, lived by the brutal law of the tooth. It is also true that this did not seem to deter the rats of the exodus from successfully adapting to the new surroundings. For them, accustomed to the systematic violence of man, that of their own kind was a lover's caress. What benefit could a soul as sensitive as mine gain from this unruly mob?

But that couldn't be the end of my journey. Not chaos and degradation. It wasn't by chance that these sewers were also laid out like a maze. And where there is a maze, there is always—I repeat, always—a point from which to infer the solution. Obviously it was in that maze that my reward was waiting for me.

To escape notice I covered my fur with slime, and I assumed a dull and anonymous expression, after which I set out. I took the first left and the second right, and then again and again. But my efforts were in vain. Apparently in this place no direction made more sense than any other. No amount of distance covered led to anything. Using reason was no help. In that broth it was impossible to discern forms, substances or values. Everything had been corrupted into decadent triviality, fatuous uniformity, garbage. At last I reached a drainpipe that was discharging a dense concentration of printed pages, periodicals, bindings. I tried to climb up to the source of this knowledge. I spied the opening and made my way up the conduit down which it was pouring. And I found myself in the . . . university library.

I set up camp there. I spent about a month in this peaceful reflective place, leading the life of a bookworm in complete solitude, roaming far and wide in that immense maze of corridors, ideas and theories. In a short while I devoured all the great works of Western civilization, leaving aside only the hardest bindings.

The big questions continued to torture me. The whole universe seemed nothing but a series of mazes that led only to other mazes: plumbing, hallways, canals, streets. How far would I have to travel before I found a way out? All the routes seemed the same. They all curved back on themselves, they had no beginning or direction or end. I kept on searching. But I ran into other mazes: the subway, the street system, water mains, air vents . . . And yet I was certain there was a place where I would be freed from that endless cycle of going back and forth. I knew that when I finally stuck my nose in that place, I would find Revelation, Deliverance, the Summum Bonum.

Once again I took the first left and the second right. And again and again.

One day at last, while I was downheartedly making my way along a drainage ditch as dark as my soul, I spied an unusual murine form hanging from the ceiling pipes. It was a winged rodent with a mysterious air, and its behavior was as strange as its physiognomy. It was upside down, facing me, and its unblinking eyes seemed to be indicating something, giving me a direction. Apparitions of this kind have their raison d'être. I put myself in the same upside-down position. I observed and I reasoned. Thanks to this reversal of my outlook and to the increased blood flow to my brain, the solution was immediately revealed to me. Its elegance was evident: from that *exact* point it would be enough to take the first left and the second right, the first left and the second right . . . All the way to my destination, the Place, Topos.

And so it was.

It was only a question of time until, as I foresaw, I reached the way out. I followed it, pressing on until the light dazzled me.

And I easily found the way into the Department.

"From the tag on his neck I'd say he's one of ours," one of the researchers said. "But the data have become unreadable."

"Put him through the tests again."

So that is how I came to reside very close to where I'd started from. In the cage next door.

I didn't have to wait long for the Great Reward to make her entrance. Her coat and eyes were as bright as Revelation, as dazzling as Knowledge. Ljuba came up to me with little steps, curling her tail, slithering, stretching her body hair by hair, hesitating. How beautiful she was! She was as seductive as an intuition, as disconcerting as an antiphrasis, as shy as truth. Stupid as a poem.

"I am V-I-S-K-O-V-I-T-Z," I explained to her.

And What Did She Say, Viskovitz?

With Ljuba it was love at first sight. She was the most beautiful parrot of the Caribbean. So I went to call on her without a second thought. I looked into her eyes and said, "I love you."

"I love you," she replied. It was the beginning of a great passion. Our love nest was the whole jungle, the mad ardor of youth was burning under our feathers, the sky itself wasn't big enough to hold it. We sang, we danced, we made love to the rhythm of the rumba, the mambo, the conga, the merengue. So one day I made up my mind and asked her, "Will you marry me?"

"Will you marry me?" she shot back.

"Of course, my love."

"Of course, my love," she answered.

So I built the most beautiful nest in the archipelago, and there we spent our honeymoon. Holding her close, I said to her, "I'd like to have children."

She replied that she would like to have them, too. Two of them were born—darling children—never a cross word, never disobedient, always ready to return our affection.

What else could anyone want from life?

Some sort of surprise. And so I began seeing another she-parrot. One day I confessed to Ljuba. I said to her, "I have a lover."

"I have a lover," she replied.

"My lover is Lara," I continued.

"My lover is Lara," she confessed.

What could I say to that? I was dumb as stone. My wife with my lover. If you put it like that it could seem almost like good news, but it soon became clear that this triangle couldn't go on. But I went to Ljuba and said, "Choose. Either me or her."

"Her," she answered.

Then I went to Lara and delivered the same ultimatum. "Either me or her!"

"Her!"

"Damn you," I said.

"Damn you," she squeaked back.

And What Did She Say, Viskovitz?

I was completely fed up with being the butt of these refrains. Was it possible that life ran along such superficial plot lines? How could I get past this predicament? In my desperation I decided to seek the advice of an enlightened mind, a parrot who had gained renown as a master of wisdom and as a spiritual guide.

"Master," I blurted out. "What can we do to get beyond these cut-rate answers, to escape this humdrum, this mediocrity? Tell me, master, what must we do?"

"Do," the sage answered.

THE LESS SAID, THE BETTER, VISKOVITZ

Our leader, who was also our teacher, always said to us, "You can tell a well-behaved fish by his language. He is never vulgar, he always looks you straight in at least one eye and, above all, he always tells the truth."

He was telling us this as he swam along his complex route, alternating the rhythm of the strokes of his tail and of his dorsal fin, because dance is the only way in which most fish can communicate. A language ill adapted to those who are impatient or short of breath. He would then catch my eye and inevitably add, "Viskovitz, repeat what I just said."

I would answer that question with silence. Life had already taught me that silence is the only way a fish can tell the truth and tell it politely. And I was a well behaved fish. I'll try to explain myself better.

If, to say the word "hydroelectric," you have to rise and sink in the water six times and touch your anal fin with a gill, it is ichthyologically impossible to keep looking at your interlocutor. Moreover, there is little likelihood that the meaning of your movements will be understood by him. Perhaps he will take them to mean "eel" and be offended. It's nobody's fault, it's the fault of language, and it is thence all the problems of us fish arise. Take my name—Viskovitz. It requires approximately ten minutes to pronounce it correctly. Eventually I used it as an exercise to lose weight. And there was also this: it could be mistaken for "Certainly, if it's okay with your cousin," or "Kiss me all over, nymph," or even something like "A mathematical series is perfect when each term is the limit of a progression or of a regression and each progression and regression contained in the series has a limit within the series itself."

The confusion is increased by the fact that there are as many languages as there are schools of fish and as many dialects as there are fish. That not only makes it difficult to speak but equally difficult to be silent. Even a simple act like swallowing a cuttlefish could be misunderstood; someone could see it as a metaphor. In some cultures the black ink of the cuttlefish represents "evil," "deceit," "the illusoriness of life." The cuttlebone, on the other hand, "soul" or "purity." That's why I only eat herring and prefer to chew them far from a crowd.

At the root of all the fragmentation that characterizes ocean life is the difficulty of teaching language to a fish. I'll explain myself better. If you point with your mouth at a sole and then with your body draw an "S" in the water, your pupil will usually understand that "S" means sole. You can do the same with a herring, gudgeon or a spiny lantern fish. But try to use the same system to explain to that fish the concept of "incommensurability" or "classicalness" or simply "truth." The fish will swear that he gets it, but you can be sure that he understands something quite different, like "low tide," "diver" or "tiny bubbles."

My kids always asked me, "Papa, how are fish born?"

To that question I replied with silence. There are those who pride themselves on finding the right words in those delicate situations and on being able to speak in a natural tone of voice. Easier done than said.

I mean I wasn't even dreaming of explaining certain things—it would have taken months. I simply picked the first female in heat who happened along and showed the kids how it's done, even though I already had a large family. Because among fish, at least among us sticklebacks, sex is never embarrassingly intimate or daring. The female lays eggs in the nest, and the male fertilizes them without even touching her. It is enough for him to look at her color and to delight in the little dance she does for him. Actually it's not even necessary for there to be a female. Studies conducted by humans have demonstrated that her image on a cardboard cutout is enough to get a male to fertilize the eggs. Even if the eggs aren't really there. Not only that—we continue to incubate the nonexistent eggs and oxygenate them with our tails. This doesn't mean we're stupid, mind you. It means that nature prefers to err on the side of plenty rather than on the side of scarcity. If sex and reproduction didn't respond to an innate language and were left to the misunderstandings of fish language, fish would think that you're talking about Cuban dances or I don't know what. Naturally there are extreme cases, like that of Zucotic, who has given names and an extensive education to those nonexistent fish. But that is truly a case at the far end of the spectrum.

In any case, a good rule with one's own children is to communicate as little as possible, limiting oneself to simple precepts such as "Don't say vulgar things—it's easier to just do them." Or "Don't make up lies—you might accidentally tell the truth." Or "Never say, 'Look out, friend, it's a hook'—it's easier to find a new friend."

My female companion had the bad habit of asking, "Do you love me, Viskovitz?"

To that question I replied with silence.

Because you're never sure if that is even the question. If whoever is asking it is a walrus or a polyp, you can rule out love because of the context. But even if the speaker is a mother of your children, you're better off not getting involved in a precise answer, because if whoever has coupled with you is someone who comes from another school, "love" for her surely means something different, like "scratch my swim bladder" or I don't know what. Conversely, if she asks you to scratch her swim bladder, she may actually want a lot more from you, and you're better off not assuming that responsibility.

Take for instance my first wife, Lara. She came from another atoll, and when I met her she didn't even know what I meant if I said "sardine." So I had to teach her everything, starting with concepts like "good" and "bad," "fish" and "crustacean." After which I proceeded to more recent idiomatic usages and to archaic expressions that retained a certain poetic value. One day after a year of marriage, just to make conversation, I tossed out, "There's a certain guy in our school, Zucotic, who suffers from seasickness. What do you think of that?"

And she: "Yoga lessons? No, I don't think they'd do you any good."

Perplexed, I tried to change the subject, hazarding an innocuous "It's a bit cool this evening, dear."

And she: "Caviar? No, I'm against abortion."

Then I understood that our whole love story had been a misunderstanding. At last I had an explanation for those many looks charged with hate, and others with bursts of love. And for that strange story of the grandfather who escaped from a sardine tin. I decided it would be better for us to separate, and to avoid further misunderstandings, I moved to a different ocean.

Then I got fished out and ended up in an aquarium. It was only there that things began to go better. It was there that I met my last wife, Ljuba, the most understanding of my female companions, the least ambiguous. At first we had our difficulties: her perfect beauty made me a little insecure, kept me in awe of her. Then, thanks to her patience, we overcame them. With time we worked out our perfect code of communication, made up of small gestures and long pauses.

I remember the day she opened her soul to me. I'd come up to her with a pirouette, as if to say, "I caress you with my mind. What deep enchantment binds me to you? I put my faith in your bewitching scales, I find in your tuna profile the secret of infinite sweetness." She answered me with a languid and imperceptible movement of her tail, which could mean many things, but which I interpreted as "Never hold back, my love. My existence doesn't enjoy peace but rather sexual ravening and freedom from all conventions." So then I did something rare for a fish—I kissed her.

From that day, from that moment when I understood she was a cardboard cutout, our relationship became more serene, communication less burdensome and the sex fantastic.

You're a Prickly Fellow, Viskovitz

Being born is never a pleasant experience, but for us it was a particularly ugly fifteen minutes. After she gave birth to us, Mama looked at us with disgust. Her first words to us were "Accursed monsters! Works of Satan! Vile creatures!" Then, lifting her claws to heaven, "Curse, Oh Higher Power, this unworthy offspring, and curse their seed! Cleanse your creation of their obscenity! May the Evil One take pity on them!"

Not exactly the sort of encouragement you expect from a mother. From a mom you expect some sort of arachnid affection, you expect her to carry you piggyback the way moms usually do with their little scorpions. You expect an upbringing. You don't expect her to spit on you and disappear forever in a cloud of sand, leaving you to fry your postabdomen on the desert floor. She was so lacking in family feeling that she hadn't even given us first names. Only last names: Viskovitz, Zucotic, Petrovic and Lopez.

It's no wonder we didn't really consider ourselves brothers and that we soon decided to cast our lots separately. We pointed our pincers in opposite directions. Petrovic went north, Lopez south, and Zucotic to the east. I, Viskovitz, followed the path of the sun and set off to win the west.

All the while I was asking myself, "How will I make it in a competitive place like the world without a family or an education?"

Mom had given birth to us right in the middle of the Mojave Desert, one of the hottest and most arid climates in North America. The surface temperature was over 140 degrees Fahrenheit, and the relative humidity was near zero. A place where you couldn't afford to shed tears.

Suddenly the tarsal hairs of my eight legs felt the vibrations of a gigantic animal who was moving toward me, one who in all likelihood wanted my death.

A shame it's over already, I said to myself, a shame that my birth was nothing but a waste of time. We arachnids aren't whiners the way mammals are, but my first impulse was to find the abdomen of a nonexistent mom and whimper. Then I tried to hightail it out of there. But something wasn't working. My legs, instead of following the signals of my cerebral ganglia, were carrying my sorry ass the wrong way, just where I didn't want to go—toward suicide. Was it possible I was that clumsy? I popped up right under the nose of the monster, and there I watched in astonishment as my little body performed a series of lightning-fast moves over which I had no control. In the end, the beetle was stretched out on the ground, paralyzed with venom, my tail planted in his skull. He was still moving his antennae, but I'd already begun to suck up his lymph and eat his appendages.

So who was I? The answer is obvious: a predator, a savage beast programmed to kill. With a shudder of terror I realized I had no power over the firing of my reflexes, over those savage instincts. Was I a monster?

Two days later, while I was still stripping the flesh from my prey, I was visited by another scorpion, a mean hombre at least two inches long with a cocksure attitude.

He hissed, "I don't cotton to your hunting in my territory, snot-nose. Let loose of that-there beetle and vamoose."

In those two days I'd grown a lot, but not enough to get sassy with someone like that. It was one of those situations where you ought to put your tail between your legs and lower your claws.

I was about to say, "Excuse me, sir, I was just born a little while ago. I didn't know this was your territory. I beg your pardon." But the voice that came out of my spines actually sounded like this: "I don't like the way you're talking to me, stranger. Let's see if your tail is as fast as your mouth." Once again my body was disobeying me and I saw myself going forward in fighting position, my claws swinging and my tail cocked. With my lateral ocelli I saw a group of termites gather around us to watch the duel. What could I do? Nothing. Nothing but stand there watching myself like those peons, hoping my instincts knew how to do their job. My adversary made the first move, but his tail was still in midair when mine was injecting its poison.

"You'll go far, kid," the loser said with his last breath. "What do folks call you?"

"The name is Viskovitz," I breathed. I left the carcass to the scavengers, wiped off my tail and instinctively cut a notch in its first segment. "God Almighty, Viskovitz," I said. "Good God Almighty."

That duel was the first in a long series. Each time a scorpion came along who was too big for his britches, calling himself boss of the territory that I was passing through, then each time my tail made it come out the other way. This useless bloodshed wouldn't have been necessary if I'd been a stay-at-home, but I had itchy feet and couldn't help going wherever they carried me. It got to be so no one dared to cross my path. One day I noticed this two-clawed hombre keeping his distance. I heard him say to his kid, "Look, son. There goes Viskovitz—the fastest tail in the west."

The desert folks began to come to me to right wrongs and break up fights, and there were quite a few who would pay any price in prey or territory to get on my good side. What I wanted most of all was to put my tail on the side of justice. So, when the good old Earp brothers asked me to help them protect their little snot-rag of land from the designs of the high and mighty Ewing boys, I was glad to take their side. That set-to got to be kind of famous. After I took care of the Ewings' hired killers, one after the other, I faced off with the Ewings themselves near Boot Hill. I got rid of all four of them at one go. Just one shot with both my claws, my tail and my mandibles. If it had ended up that way, it would've been something to be proud of. But when the Earp brothers, all fired up on account of winning, came to thank me . . . I took them out, too. All of them in one shot, with both my claws, my tail and my mandibles.

It tore my heart out to watch them die. One of them said to me, "You can't do a thing about it, scorpio. It's just the way you are. You're a crude life form, a *Paruroctonus mesaensis*. You get to go on living on account of the speed of your killer reflexes. You wouldn't be so fast if you could think about what you're doing. All it takes is a nothing—a vibration in the critical zone around you—and zak! Your blind reflexes just lash out. It's the madness of this ecosystem that creates an uncontrollable and stupid machine like you, Viskovitz."

That was pretty much the truth of it. I was a stranger in my own body, helpless before the automatism of my primitive nervous system. I shed a tear and cursed my fate. It came to me at last that the one good thing I could do for folks was to keep far away. That was why the Good Lord had put me in the desert—so I'd do the least harm to His creatures.

But pretty soon I reached sexual maturity and my feet got to taking me where there was the highest concentration of female pheromones. One day I came across a whole bunch of them coming from a real pretty pink scorpion called Lara. She had a nice curvy abdomen and a cute little pear-shaped telson. She came up to me, all skittish. She wanted to cozy up to me. "Don't be afraid, Visko," she simpered. "Sexual pheromones inhibit the predatory reflex."

So I went on up till I was just about touching her. For the first time a living being was right there in my critical zone and kept on living. For the first time I felt the breath of another arachnid, the heat of her metabolism. It was a miracle; my killer instincts had been tamed by love and beauty. I felt the need to communicate to her all the throbbing of my soul, all the tenderness of my feelings, but the only thing I managed to express was a rough and all too short discharge of my copulatory reflexes. Which missed the target.

"Sorry," I mumbled. "I guess I'm not as good at this stuff as with my tail."

"These things happen. We scorpions are rather crude arthropods. You'll see, it'll get better with time."

"With time? And what'll happen if the sexual attraction falls off? The killer instinct will come back."

"It won't fall off. You'll see. And I don't believe this killer instinct is something that can't be cured. I want to live with you, Visko, raise your children and grow old beside you."

For a moment I saw my life in this new light. I would be a responsible head of a family, I'd keep my tail under control and live in harmony with the community. Sundays I'd go to church and not kill anyone during the sermon, and God would bless me.

"Okay, Lara. Let's do it. Lara?" I thought she'd fallen asleep. Only later did I realize she had my stinger planted in her skull. Our relationship hadn't stood the test of time.

Figuring it was the proper thing to do, I carried her body to her family. In my desert vocabulary I tried to find some words of condolence and apology, but all I managed to do was massacre her parents and rape her sister. I really wasn't made for social life.

That episode was only the first disappointment in a wretched emotional life marked by the failure of every attempt at building a stable affectionate relationship, a family. Every time the script was the same. There always came that day when I'd come home from hunting and find my darlings massacred by some low-down varmint. Then I would swear vengeance on their tomb and set out on the trail of the killers. But every time those tracks came around in a circle. They led to me. I was the low-down varmint, the brutal executioner. Facing the evidence of my crimes, I raised my tail over my own head. In vain. The word "suicide" wasn't in my genetic vocabulary. My killer reflexes mocked me. Who could put an end to those horrors and render justice?

We scorpions are at the top of the food chain, so I couldn't hope to be killed by a predator. Only a tail faster than mine could punish me for my sins. Fortunately, because of my crimes—the rapes and murders I continued to commit—there was a price on my head. Bounty hunters began to show up. The best tails in the territory got together in bands of vigilantes and set out after me. Day after day, as I was splitting their skulls, I kept on hoping that someone with the right stuff would step up. Maybe one of my brothers. Or maybe that father I'd never known—the one who'd raped my mother and started this curse.

But one day I saw a very different figure appear on the horizon. She was black as poison, fiery as hate, beautiful as death. She came down from the dune, silent as a mirage, slithering like a kootch dancer. Swinging her tarsi and flexing her chitinous plates like a queen of the desert, she advanced with the malice of a carnivorous phantom. She stopped five lengths from me. She rested the spines of her pedipalps on her tarsi and leveled four of her lobster eyes at me.

"Don't kid yourself," she hissed. "I'm here to kill you."

Her scent put me in a daze and disarmed every one of my defensive reflexes. Her bewitching spell paralyzed me like the poison that rivets the prey before the coup de grâce. I had finally found what I was looking for: my defeat. The moment had come to welcome the end with gratitude. And yet in that moment my will to live had never been stronger. In those instants as never before my existence had meaning. And then there was this: what use would my death be if this diabolical temptress lived on, this exterminating machine even more murderous than I?

That thought gave me the rage I needed to cock my tail and get into my fighting stance.

We stayed still, staring at each other with cold eyes that were devoid of all consciousness, our bodies entirely given over to the one power they knew—the law of the tail, the law of the West. There followed a long silence, broken only by the scuttling feet of spiders, mites and other insects who gathered in a circle to watch that ritual as old as the desert. The whistling of the wind was sinister, like a *dejuello*, a song of death.

Then there was the vibration that our killer reflexes were waiting for.

Our bodies hurtled against each other and . . . in a state of amazement we watched them while they caressed each other, while they entwined in a tender and explosive embrace.

Afterward it was the huntress who was more embarrassed.

"I've never been so humiliated, this has never happened to me . . . I hate you, Viskovitz."

"And I don't like you, either. But you can call me Visko."

"I . . . I am Ljuba," she whispered.

In the hours, the days, that followed, we repeated this duel over and over, always with the same result. A tie. The winner was going to be whoever got tired of the other first. Ljuba was convinced it would happen to her, and she kept on jumping up against me to prove it—to the point of making me rather tired of her, and I ended up hitting her with my tail but with so little energy it seemed a caress. It went on like this for weeks until one day I said to her, "Ljuba, by now it's clear that we have a crude form of passion for each other and that we don't really want to see each other dead. So it would be better for both of us to separate before someone really gets hurt."

"I think you're right. But what about the babies?"

"Babies? We'd be better off killing them as soon as they're born."

Ljuba gave birth to a little girl as black and mean as her and a little boy with a lively tail who looked just like me. It might have been that resemblance, or something to do with their scent, but I just couldn't bring myself to come down on them with my tail. Each time I went to kill them, a discharge of involuntary reflexes made me carry them piggyback, sing them ballads and worry about their education.

Every day at dawn, as I watched Ljuba tuck the babies into the sand to preserve their moisture, I felt a horror. The first time they began to whimper, we would probably kill them. And if we ever disappointed them, they would kill us. Sooner or later somebody would lose patience.

Every evening I came home with my heart in my throat, expecting the worst. Other times I surprised myself by wishing for it, praying for the catastrophe.

But day after day, month after month, life went on peacefully. The babies went on growing up healthy, slaughtering their schoolmates. Ljuba and I went on adoring each other, massacring the next-door neighbors. Everything went on in perfect harmony, and there was no way to escape this intolerable, sinister happiness.

You've Made a Bad Name for Yourself, Viskovitz

It's not an advantage to be named Viskovitz when the little life has to offer is handed out in alphabetical order. In our anthill that was the way they nourished us larvae. The only one worse off than me was Zucotic.

In return for giving us nectar, the nannies wanted our sugary fluid. Relationships were an exchange of secretions, not of affection. Because of this malnutrition and disillusion, my organs were atrophying. When I tried easing my hunger pangs by sucking my own exudations, day by day I found them more acid and bitter.

Take it from me—a larva with declining secretions is

the most despised of all creatures. They began to say to me, "You're rotten, Viskovitz." "You're disgusting." Or "You're a zero." These are words that are very hurtful.

So one day I said, "It's time to get moving, Zuco. It's time to do something."

"Do something?"

It's not an easy concept to grasp for a larva without legs, wings or sex.

"Precisely," I said. "We have to plan our future, take our fate in our own tarsi."

"Tarsi?"

"Figure of speech! We'll make do with our mammiform prominences—our bulgy parts. We'll use our orifices if we have to. The important thing is that we get to the royal larva nursery. If we eat that nectar we'll become queens, brother, and we'll rule the world. The gruel they feed us here isn't even food enough to make us asexual worker ants. We'll stay larvae the rest of our lives, Zuco. Have I made myself clear?"

"I wouldn't mind staying a larva, Visko. However things go, I'll always be an ant. So it's better to keep on being a formless plasm. I believe it's just for that reason that fate put me here and gave me this name."

How could I reason with that acephalous creature? Contracting every fiber and gripping every bump with my buccal apparatus, I dragged myself to the way out of the chamber. Then, sticking myself onto the walls with my fluids, I began to climb, to gain the first millimeters of my progress up the social scale. After a week of those furious gymnastics I was exhausted and famished, but I reached the chambers of the upper story. I collapsed on the floor, panting and moribund.

My dehydrated body didn't have any secretions to barter for food, but some larvae agreed to release a little something to me in exchange for the story of my adventure. Restored, I abruptly fell into a deep sleep, but what I'd eaten wasn't royal jelly, and when I woke up I found myself with legs but no crown. I had a horny exoskeleton, and my scythe-like mandibles were weapons. I was a soldier.

At the first assembly, when I had a chance to observe myself alongside the fellows in my unit, I was rather disappointed. Malnutrition had harmed me in a conspicuous way. Entire somites of my body were atrophied and deformed. The overall effect was that I was an underdeveloped little guy. I was a gnome. Ranked by height, I was once again the next to last, if you count the regimental mascot, an aphid.

But the more serious harm was the atrophy of the scent glands, the most important organs for an ant. An ant without an odor is an ant without identity, without an anthill. He is the most insignificant of creatures, a useless meaningless being even by ant standards. He is a zero.

I soon realized that no one was speaking to me or sharing food with me. They only noticed me when they bumped into me, and sometimes not even then. Not infrequently they came to bury me, thinking I was a corpse.

"Damn it, Visko," they would say to me then, "if you're such a wreck while we're at peace, what'll you be when there's a war!"

But when a war broke out with the neighboring anthill, it was soon apparent that the enemy didn't notice me, either. For them I wasn't even an insect. I didn't exist. Ah, if only I'd been tall enough to reach them with my mandibles. I got a nickname: "the unknown soldier." Aphids and springtails laughed at me. Even the embryos.

One evening, I ate some soporific fungi, and, hidden behind a clump of dust, I tried in vain to rest. I breathed noisily to convince myself of my existence. Then I prayed in silence. I wasn't asking for love, because I knew I was an insect without sex or hormones. I wasn't aspiring to intellectual fulfillment—I was a soldier. And I wasn't seeking communion with the fat god who sprayed insecticide. And certainly not worldly pleasures. No. I was asking for power.

The power to master the world and to enslave my neighbor, to humiliate and destroy every creature bigger than a micron, to transform every desire into a decree, every whim into a verdict. That thought was the only thing that kept me going.

I devised a plan. Being small increased my ability to concentrate and synthesize. In me there was literally no room for sentiments or scruples. I was a lowlife, predisposed by nature for every sort of villainy. My lack of odor made me, for all practical purposes, invisible. I could go into any anthill whatsoever without being stopped, and I could acquire the odor of any ant by rubbing myself on his abdomen. Dead ants could readily be used for this purpose. My handicaps would become my weapons.

It all happened very quickly. I shuffled between the rival anthill and ours and became a spy, revealing the military secrets of each side to the other. My disclosures determined the outcome of the battles and caused me to rise rapidly in the hierarchy of each army and in the esteem of the respective queens. So one day I found myself the commander in chief of both forces. I decided to let the victor be the anthill in which I was known by the name of Viskovitz. The queen of the betrayed anthill was killed and its people enslaved. With the aid of certain of its slaves, I put together a conspiracy to kill my queen. Then I had the other conspirators arrested and killed. I declared martial law and assumed all civil power.

The next day I proclaimed myself emperor.

At that point I was the most powerful insect in the known world. My every word was law, my every deed history. On that throne I could complete the conquest of the planet, or create a new civilization—abolishing castes, trophic castration, the extermination of males—thereby changing the course of history and the entire evolution of the species.

But it is a given that an ant lives only a few months. And it was also a given that the fat god had gone on vacation and left a loaf of dry bread on the table. I decided that the energies of my people would be better employed building a colossal monument to me. It would be an imperishable testimony to my Myrmidonian greatness, the work that would make me gigantic and immortal. I myself directed the construction at the same time as I posed, my hind legs slightly bent and my gaze fixed on the horizon. Every other activity was suspended and all individuals summoned to take part in the work. Those incapable were sacrificed, and their bodies used as cement in the construction. The jaws of the soldiers sculpted the shape in the bread, the worker ants carried away the soft white parts and the dead bodies. I posed patiently, fanned and perfumed by slaves.

The miracle was almost finished. My deep-felt satisfaction began to appear in the expression of the statue that portrayed me. It was all true: those long, jointed antennae, that immense mesothorax—they were mine. This masterpiece was my second metamorphosis; I felt my soul transfer itself into that perfect and indestructible body. It was the apex of my triumph.

Only one thing was missing: Zucotic.

I found him in the same malodorous underground chamber in which I'd left him. Eating almost nothing, he'd managed to postpone metamorphosis. He remained a larva. He was a senile wrinkled baby, an opaque clot of acidic lymph and resignation. You had to see him to believe it.

"Infancy is over, Zuco. It's time to grow your little feet and walk."

"I'd rather stay here, Visko. I'm at peace with myself. The bit of food I take is offered freely. I'm not a burden on the community."

"This isn't advice, Zuco. It's an order. I'd like to see the face you'll make when you have one. Is it possible you don't realize how ridiculous you are? They give you charity because you're a clown, because they can laugh at you and feel superior."

"And yet there must be something of value if the emperor has deigned to come see me. It would astonish you to learn that people come here not to mock me but to ask my advice—"

"That's enough," I snapped. "Guards, feed this creature. And feed it with royal jelly, I want it to become a queen."

They forced the nectar down his gullet, but the metamorphosis didn't take place. His wilted membranes couldn't take the strain and his body burst like a boil, oozing its yellowish contents onto the ground.

"Did you know him, Your Majesty?" the chief of staff asked.

"General, he was my best friend."

"I'm very sorry, Your Highness."

"I, on the other hand, am not," I replied, irritated. "What difference does one friend make when I can have millions of slaves?"

The inauguration was two days later. Throughout the empire the calendars were reset to zero. My people gathered in front of the Colossus on their knees. The priests chanted the "Ode to the Emperor," and I, Viskovitz, I the great, marched up to the podium and turned to the crowd.

"Citizens of the empire," I thundered. "This extraordinary work of engineering genius is a monument to greatness itself. I mean exactly that—to greatness. Because greatness, ladies and gentlemen, isn't something measured in millimeters. Greatness is measured in centuries! Anything that has value outlasts time. And in the judgment of time, ladies and gentlemen, great is the ant and small are the dinosaurs . . . Today more than ever, my children, I am sure of one thing: when all the animal species that now exist are extinct, we will still be here— building anthills. And, admiring this statue, we will cry out, 'Who would have said it? The greatest of all was Viskovitz!'"

"Hurrah! Long live the emperor!"

It was then that I heard the crack. It might have been the ovation or the tramping feet of the people. The two hind legs of the monument had given way and the Colossus had settled on its abdomen.

"Shall we suspend the ceremony, Your Immensity?" my vizier asked.

"No. Let it go on," I ordered. The damage was irreparable. Who would manage to relift that boulder? There was only one thing to do.

I bent over, reached back with my mandible and cut cleanly. I, too, sank onto my abdomen. It was extraordinary—I felt no pain. And once again the resemblance was perfect.

"Greatness, my people—" I shouted, drowning the cries.

Crack.

Another three legs had snapped. Now there was only one propping up the construction.

I did what I had to do.

"Greatness," I shrieked, balancing on my last leg, "is not—"

Thump.

The crowd began to flee in every direction. The collapsing sculpture had broken into three truncated sections. The head and the thorax had shattered, but the large oval shape of the abdomen had stayed intact and was rolling toward me. It wasn't the idea of dying that bothered me so much as the shape of that abdomen. It looked like a larva. It was a statue of Zucotic that was killing me, not a statue of me. It wasn't the portrait of an emperor that I was leaving to history. It was the portrait of a nothing.

Who Do You Think You Are, Viskovitz?

"Who am I?" I asked myself. Not finding an answer, I asked my father.

"Depends on the context," he explained. "We chameleons are like the pause between two words."

"And . . . our personality?"

"Why settle for one personality, kid, when you can have them all? Where does it get you to be yourself when, just by pretending to be someone else, you can seduce really fantastic lizards, get good marks at school, make your rivals run away? Follow my example: today I'm your pop; tomorrow, who knows?"

It was always the same story. All you had to do was remix the colors a little, inflate the pulmonary branches and you could look like whomever you wanted . . . Of course that meant you couldn't trust anyone, not even relatives. It wasn't an accident that in our family we all had names that ended with a question mark. I was called Viskovitz?

"I don't know what to believe in anymore, Dad. I'm confused."

"Good for you, son. If you're confused, you've got it made as a chameleon. It's better that the secret of our existence doesn't get out, Visko? Most of all to certain serpents. Now get moving—it's time to go to school."

"School? What the hell am I going to do there? The only subject is 'Our Native Tongue.' And the first lesson is how to hold it."

"Fine. That way you'll learn to express yourself without getting in my face."

"Dad, let me tell you that when it comes to oral expression, a good kiss is better than all those hours at school."

"I don't want to hear you talking about kisses, Visko? They're dangerous, they'll tie you up. It's better not to get mixed up with girls."

"Oh, fine—and if you've fallen in love?"

"Well, then you're in trouble, son. It's the worst thing that could happen to a chameleon."

"Did it ever happen to you?"

He thought a bit, raising a flexible eye toward his crest. "Yes. Even I fell in love once. But I have to say, I never understood with whom. And then I never succeeded in telling her apart from the background. And then I got terribly jealous. If someone brushed a branch, I thought he was feeling up her prehensile tail. If he licked dew from a leaf, I thought he was sucking her ear. If he sighed over the view . . . well, I saw the worst implications. Luckily, love is a thermal phenomenon, Visko?, and we cold-blooded animals only have to worry about it between 11 a.m. and 2 p.m."

I had had enough of the cynicism of that old lizard—and who knows if he really was my father. I said my good-byes and lowered myself by way of a hanging root. At the shrub level I melted into the selaginella and the zinziber-ace. I kept on past the water-lily pond until I reached the tree of the chameleon I loved. I stealthily climbed the trunk of a cauliflore palmetto, carefully managing my mimicry so I wouldn't give myself away—and then I was blessed with a vision of her. She was indeed visible. She was gazing at herself in the water gathered in a hollow leaf of an epiphyte and, humming, was peeling off her skin in a slow striptease, while her body, rather than mimicking, was inventing fantastic colors. Hidden behind a saprophytic orchid, I landed a furtive kiss dead center. I wondered if I was the only one doing this. Then I spread my tongue on a branch, hoping she'd lie down on it.

She called out, "Who's there?" Perhaps I'd made a noise.

"Visko?" I admitted, leaving out the "vitz," because if you pronounce letters like "T," "L," "D," "N" or "Z" with a dry throat, there's always the chance your sticky tongue will stay stuck to the roof of your mouth.

"And what do you want?" she hissed. With one independent eye she continued to look at her reflection, while with the other she looked me in the eye that was looking her in the eye that was looking at me. I told her the truth. I told her I'd been enchanted by her cutaneous chromatophores, and I wondered how she managed to be so creative with her scales. She smiled at me.

"It's not hard," she answered. "To be original you have to go back to the origins, lizard. The secret of being oneself is knowing how to give up on it. Empty yourself, and let yourself fill back up. If you know how to do that, *voilà,* your colors will start to speak to each other, and instead of a question mark at the end of that ridiculous name, you'll be able to put an exclamation point. I am Ljuba!" She pronounced that difficult name without hesitation, snapping her tongue like a whip. Then, unexpectedly, she said, "Want to go for a stroll?"

I froze. "A stroll?"

"Yes, it's the mating season and you'll do as well as any other . . . Come here." I couldn't believe my luck. A slime like me with that arboreal fairy! I went closer and discovered that my colors imitated hers: vermilion, turquoise, poppy red; marbled, speckled, pebbled! *"Caramba!"* I said to myself. "This must be bliss." She was completely different from my pale schoolmates. For her I would climb mountains, I would face vipers and civets. And if she were to get mixed up with the background, so what—seeing her scales everywhere, I would love every leaf, every sunset, every flower. And to each one I would give that unpronounceable name "Llljuba!"

I dove into that rainbow. I caressed her dermal lobes and I clung to her crest. I let myself be carried away by her undulations and I sank into oblivion, drowning in her viscid exudations, adoring every millimeter of those scales. WHUMP. We fell off the branch and plummeted onto the thorns of a whistling acacia.

Ah well. The next day I discovered that my stupid ex-girlfriend Lara had the same wounds, and so did my sickly and repressed deskmate Jana. They were the same chameleon!

It was then that I lost my last certainties.

And it is there that I finally found myself. But I didn't recognize me.

You've Found Peace at Last, Viskovitz

In my heart was only nothingness and beatitude.

My mind, having destroyed the armor of the ego, being free of desire, memories and karmic impulses, was focused in the greatest meditative absorption, close to a cessation of all activities, to a sublimated state of consciousness.

Transcendence, illumination, reawakening.

At that point my diamond body would have overflowed with shining prana from head to tail and I, Viskovitz, would have finally dissolved into light, the divine Atman, the Eternal Orgasm . . . But just then an unpleasant smell started swirling in my turbinate bones. A smell I thought I had buried in the past. I tried to keep my concentration, bark my mantra and visualize a mandala, but the delicate balance of the samadhi had been shattered. I painfully opened an eye. In front of me was Skittles, our spiritual master, absorbed in the peace of meditation, and all around were the monastery's other dogs, some perfectly still in their asana, others more interested in the offerings deposited on the pagoda's minor altars than in self-discovery. A German shepherd with brown fur was climbing the temple steps. I intercepted him just in time, as he was lifting his leg against the altar.

"You're in a sacred place, Zucotic!" I growled. He was a police dog, and I knew full well that his training did not include any type of spiritual education. I, too, had worn that collar.

"Long time no see, you old wolf," he barked, and joyously sniffed my butt. He talked about the old times, when we had worked together in Narcotics. Then he told me that he had come to ask my advice, to discuss something that was bothering his conscience.

I cut him off. "I've lost interest in moral questions."

"I beg you. You're the only dog I respect. You have always been the wisest of the pack, the one with the best nose . . ." I let him talk. It seemed that Korzybski, his handler, had pocketed some powder. Not one or two small bags—three big kilos of China white. "We're talking heroin, Visko, Satan's flour, the Big Shit . . ." He kept shaking his large head as if he wanted to rid himself of it; he was panting, yipping, and I was afraid he would start howling right in the middle of the pagoda. "What should I do, Visko? I'm the only one who knows he buried those bags in his garden."

Poor Zucotic. Personally, I had nothing against him, but he belonged to another planet, a planet whose gravitational pull I no longer felt. I, Viskovitz, was floating on a different astral plane. How could I explain it to him?

"I understand your state of mind, Zuco, but you're wasting your time talking about this with me. I stopped believing in your values years ago. Then I stopped believing in values in general, and finally I even stopped believing in believing. After which I began to dissolve into the universe . . . you can't ask the air you breathe for advice, Zuco."

"Damn it, living here really isn't good for you, you old wolf."

There wasn't much thirst for understanding in his voice. I looked at him with tenderness and ended the conversation. "I have to go now, I hope you can find peace." I turned my back and retraced my steps. When I reached the top of the stairs, I turned around and saw he was gone. Luckily he had left quietly, but from the smell I judged that what was dripping down the temple's steps wasn't holy water.

I went back and rejoined the brotherhood, sitting still and focusing my thoughts, but my mind was now disturbed by a memory. The memory of a time when I had worn a badge and been decorated for valor and vigilance, a time when I had loved a beautiful Alsatian and that Alsatian had been killed. No, this was not the day I would find the peace of nirvana.

A week had gone by. In the purifying calm of the Sangha, through the awareness of breathing and the undisturbed and detached contemplation of body and mind, I proceeded along the clear path that led to Liberation. When introducing us to the techniques of Clear Comprehension, Skittles had said to us: "In your transient body I will show you the world, the dawning of the world, the extinction of the world and the path that leads to the extinction of the world." I, Viskovitz, was progressing along that path. At first sight Skittles—a white toy poodle with remnants of a continental clip from his younger days—did not strike one as a fully accomplished spiritual guide. But whoever had the good fortune of being the recipient of his teachings, and resting in the serenity of his gaze, knew he found himself before a holy animal, a steady and imperturbable guide. We had never seen him wag his tail.

I was therefore proceeding beyond the Five Attachments toward the Seven Factors of Illumination, and I was on the verge of grasping the Four Noble Truths when . . .

. . . I caught the scent of a bitch in the air, of an Alsatian. I concentrated on the *anupasati*, but the scent grew. It continued to grow until it engulfed me, and then it yipped—

"Viskovitz?"

I huffed crossly and opened my eyes on her little face. How long since I'd been this close to an Alsatian? Two years. Since Ljuba's death. It was better that way. Why seek such an ephemeral pleasure again? I looked at her vaguely. I don't give much importance to appearances. She had a dolichocephalic snout with tawny fur, white at the masseter and the throttle; erect ears, abundant lips, a slightly ovine stop, a prominent stipes and a nose like a brown truffle. Her mantle was a smoky, brownish red, almost pink in the undercoat. Her loin was arched, her rump oblique; she was long in the shoulder, with straight nates, tight belly, chiseled hocks, full chest, wide-set stifles, perpendicular pasterns. It really was, cynologically speaking, a body that was superb in its proportions and the arrangement of its parts, exemplary in its conformation and profile.

Certainly a bitch of important genealogy and high breeding. About a year and a half old, judging by her canines.

"Viskovitz," I confirmed.

"I'm Detective Lara, from Narcotics."

She smelled my bud and I returned the favor. It's surprising, the amount of information you can get with your nose right in there. You can sniff a soul's slightest vibrations or, if you have more material inclinations, find out everything about the hormonal cycle. I recognized the clear signs of the pre-estrus. This bitch, sexually speaking, was a time bomb.

"What can I do for the law?"

"One of our agents, Detective Zucotic, has been absent for about a week. According to reliable sources, before his disappearance he was trying to establish contact with you, Viskovitz," she yelped, in a shrill little voice, almost peevish. Her eyes continued to roam over the bald patches in my coat. "If I really am talking to the former special agent Viskovitz—"

"Visko, for the pure of heart."

"I confess, I was expecting something different. I've been hearing about the feats of Investigator Viskovitz since I was a puppy, about your legendary nose, about your prowess, and now . . ." She certainly wasn't making an effort to hide her disappointment.

"Now you, too, will have a story to tell."

"Well. It wouldn't be a good ending to the story," she said. "Our hero done in by mange and ticks, reduced to picking through the garbage."

"It's called a bum's life, Officer. But some prefer it to a leash and muzzle." I briefly told her what Zucotic had said to me. I had a certain amount of experience smelling trouble, and I advised her to steer clear of this mess.

"I'm certain that Agent Zucotic will have done his duty till the end. I intend to do mine," she barked.

I was dazzled by such dedication, initiative and contempt for danger, but I couldn't help thinking that there was some hormonal itch behind her excursion out of the kennel. In one way or another, this bitch was a danger to the purity of my soul. I gave a grunt of dismissal.

As she turned her tergum she let loose a blast of hormones. You didn't have to be a psychic to know that there were plenty more where those came from. I looked at her, perplexed, while she sniffed the air in search of something she couldn't find. How could anyone be so naive?

"It's not in the air that you will find Zucotic's scent, Detective," I heard myself say. "Those kinds of traces, air scent, come from an animal's sudoriferous glands, apocritic and eccritic. They only last a few minutes. What you're interested in is the ground scent, the smell of contact left by hairs and skin particles on the ground. Or, better still, urine traces: those are the ones that last longer, several days if it doesn't rain and there isn't too much evaporation."

"I know how to follow a scent!" she growled, baring her beautiful teeth.

I gently took her to the step where Zucotic had pissed. Once again her smell hit me. It was clear that this bitch was ovulating, and pretty soon her scent would be all over Chinatown.

"For the friendship that ties me to Zucotic . . . it's probably better if I join this investigation, Officer," I yelped. "I think my, uh, cover could come in handy."

She howled something that did not penetrate my blocked nervous system, but she didn't seem to be objecting.

Trailing Zucotic was not hard for me, and while doing that I could easily chat with Lara. Or rather, listen to her tell me about herself in her piercing bark, in a state of excitement that was getting harder and harder to control. She wanted to have a career, she said, but not to satisfy her vanity. She was an idealist and she wanted to correct the evils of this world: the docking of tails, ear amputations, puppy mills, castration, municipal pounds. Her highbrow bloodline did not stop her from hating racial discrimination, pedigrees, standards of purity, dog shows. At times it was like hearing Ljuba again, when she, too, was this young and this filled with dreams and hormones. Since she wanted to have a career, I thought it would be appropriate, on the way, to teach her the ABCs of her trade, the first rudiments of tracking. I explained backtracking, off-tracking and crosstracking, and the transfer from one surface to another: asphalt, dust, lawn. I told her that once in a while it is necessary to use the mouth, where the vomero-nasal gland is, which is connected to the olfactory bulb. I pointed it out to her by sliding my tongue over hers, and already I was letting myself drift toward the folds of her coat when—

"Those little animals. Aren't they delicious?" she barked. It was her first trip out of the kennel, and she couldn't get over being amazed by the wonders of this world.

"They're rats," I explained to her. "And that evocative hill is a dump." Two rats were working on some bones. Cursing, they slunk away.

Having abandoned her attempts at professional behavior, yelping happily, Lara began to suck those bones and then buried them. Fascinated, I watched her wag her tail. How could anyone be that young? I took advantage of the break to scratch about in the garbage. It's not as depressing as it looks. There are pieces of garbage that can enrich your diet. Lara came up to me with a big thighbone in her mouth.

"I needed to sharpen my teeth. Now I'm operational. Do you think we'll be able to find Agent Zucotic's trail in the midst of all these smells?"

How could anyone be so naive?

I explained to her that it would not be necessary, that Agent Zucotic was what she was carrying in her mouth and who, thighbone aside, had already been buried.

Zucotic's death had not surprised me nor upset me. For me it was simply a chance to meditate over the laws of karma, the wheel of samsara and the transitoriness of the citta. Death was everywhere. And in every instance I, Viskovitz, died and was reborn with the universe. But for Detective Lara, that discovery had been devastating; her delicate emotional equilibrium had given way and she had started to howl as if she had been hit by a truck. She went on for hours.

I did my best to comfort her. While I explained to her that it is from death that life begins, and that in this place, in these streets, death was celebrated with life, I slipped around her, rested one paw on her coccyx and with the other lifted myself on her haunch . . .

With a jerk, she jumped forward.

"But of course! Korzybski! He's the killer," she barked. "Quickly, let's get moving. His house isn't far, and maybe we'll be able to catch him with the loot. I won't rest until I nail that bastard." She immediately set off at a trot toward Alameda and the residential section, swinging her hips.

"Where do you think you're going in that state? Don't you know that it won't take a minute for all the dogs in the neighborhood to be all over you?" I hadn't gotten the words out of my mouth when three hoods showed up with tough-guy smiles pasted on their mugs. A foxhound, a mastiff and a miniature schnauzer.

"Boy oh boy, get a load of her!" the schnauzer barked.

"What do they want, Viskovitz?"

"Guess."

"Tell them I'm on the job."

"A job is just what we're looking for, sweetheart," the foxhound sneered.

"You heard the lady. Beat it!"

"Why don't you take a powder, Gramps," the mastiff snarled.

It was clear that calm reasoning wouldn't do the trick. Nor would it be enough to show my teeth. I took care of the schnauzer with a swift kick, then sank my teeth in the foxhound's hind parts and was shaking him when the mastiff got me from behind. He was younger and bigger than me—at least a foot taller at the withers—and it would have been a lousy evening if I hadn't been a master in the art of Bushido, the Way of the Warrior. I faked the gunsel onto his back and I laid into him with my teeth. The foxhound had already slipped away. I was bleeding from an ear and I was saddened, because I hate violence.

Lara had disappeared. But not her scent. I began to gallop and caught up with her. We were now in front of Korzybski's place, a house measuring too many square feet for a K-9 cop to afford. I was exhausted.

"You're bleeding, Visko." It was the first time she had called me that. "You were so brave." She began to lick my wounds. Long, hot, lingering licks.

It seemed to me that there was only one way to find peace. One day, I said to myself, I'll be able to rise above those crude material attachments, but for the time being, go with the flow . . . wasn't that the Way of Tao after all? I was already hovering by her tail when BANG! The gunshot came from Korzybski's house.

With a start, Lara bounded forward.

"Quick, Visko, we can't let them get away!"

"Stop. They're armed," I objected. But her beautiful hindquarters had already disappeared behind the fence. It was the perfect time to turn tail and save my hide.

Another shot rang out.

Cursing, I jumped into the yard. I found an open window and tumbled into the house.

Sergeant Korzybski's body lay in its own blood on the

kitchen floor. He had a third eye on his forehead and another little hole at heart level. As if that wasn't enough, Lara was barking in his face. By the holes in the wall I judged that the damage had been done by a .45. I poked my nose around and did not like what I smelled. The two killers were short, small-boned, judging by the volume and width of their scent's dispersion cone. Their breath stank of chow mein. And there was the odor of a fresh tattoo, the dye was *cannubia* purple. You could bet that the two hired killers belonged to the Red Dragon Triad, the most powerful in Chinatown. It was another good reason to consider the case closed.

We heard the roar of an engine starting, and naturally, Lara launched herself after the car, a gray Mercedes. I followed her, since we never would have been able to catch up to them anyway. Once even she figured this out, I explained to her that it was not wise to follow live tracks right in the middle of a highway, and I steered her into a public park where it was quieter. It was sunset, and there were roses.

Once we were in that cozy sanctuary, among the wood thrush and the smell of mint, I congratulated old Viskovitz. I stretched out on the fresh grass, and faced with that sunset, I was moved like a sentimental little hound.

Lara looked into my eyes and confessed, "Oh, Visko. I can't resist. It's my instinct, it's stronger than me."

"It's only natural," I cooed. "You're a bitch in heat and I'm an attractive wolf . . . let yourself go."

"Let myself go?"

"Right, sweetheart."

With a start, Lara jumped forward and ran into the water and began swimming toward a stick that some guy had thrown in the lake. It was *that* instinct she was talking about. The atavistic and servile instinct to fetch. She retrieved the thing for the guy, and the gonzo threw it again even farther. And Lara went after it. What could I do? I dove in. When I reached her I was completely out of breath.

"See how good I am?" she barked. "I found it even underwater! No one beats me at retrieving. No stick has ever gotten away from me."

How could anyone be so naive?

I explained to her that what she had in her mouth was not a stick but a .45-caliber Luger, eight shots in the clip and one in the chamber. And I explained that it wasn't good for your health to carry the murder weapon back to the killer.

This time Lara managed to follow the car of the hired killers all the way into the heart of Chinatown, to the Garden of the Three Pagodas, where we'd started this little jaunt. The two guys had entered sacred ground and mingled with the faithful. At that point I had to warn my mate that we found ourselves before an especially sacred place, where a *Tang,* a Taoist temple, and a *Si,* a Buddhist temple, and a *Miaw,* a Confucian temple, had come together within the same perimeter. Every corner one could see had been built according to the most rigorous geomantic principles of feng shui. It was a place where you barked under your breath and you didn't show up with a bitch in heat. But Lara wouldn't listen to reason. She was convinced that the two men had the heroin Zucotic had died for, and she wanted to get it back at all costs.

When we caught up with the two killers, we found them in the company of another dozen gorillas in the Triad. There were some monks with them. They were carrying ceremonial umbrellas and a parade of offerings toward the principal altar of the *Si,* dedicated to Guan Hin, the goddess of forgiveness.

Inside those offerings there were kilos of China white.

I stopped Lara by grabbing her collar. It really wouldn't do to disturb such a devout consortium of souls. Plus, dogs were not admitted to the presence of the Goddess.

"You're well known here, Visko. You could try to attract the monks' attention."

I explained to her that even they were in cahoots with the Triad. That the drugs were hidden in the propitiatory offerings, in the wooden elephants and the porcelain dragons. And that the statues were then divvied up in the Chinese neighborhoods of other cities, always with the blessing of Guan Hin. The Triads were very generous with the divinity. They had to be if they wanted a place in heaven. The cash was in the red envelopes—and that was for the monks. I explained to her that this was none of my business. A guy can buy paradise any way he wants—even with an envelope filled with powder. Besides, the head monk was a dog lover.

"I love dogs, too, Visko, but I don't go around dealing this stuff. Damn it. I can't believe that you knew these things and didn't notify headquarters." She was overstimulated, she was shaking with indignation and nerves.

"A slice of the pie belongs to them, too, puppy," I explained to her. "Korzybski made the mistake of biting off more than he could chew. He didn't stick to the deal, and that's why they wiped him out. Years ago, when I was still on the force, Agent Ljuba and I uncovered this trail together. I can assure you that nobody in Narcotics lifted a finger. And Ljuba paid with her life."

"Ljuba. She was very beautiful, wasn't she?"

"You can say that again. She was an alpha female."

"We owe it to them, Visko."

"Huh?"

"Listen. I might not be the best detective, but I am sure of one thing: I'm not going to leave this place until I've confiscated at least a sample of that stuff. I owe it to them. To Zucotic, and to Ljuba. And you're going to help me, Viskovitz. Because you have a job to finish." With an irresistible swirl, she brushed her fur on my loins and then stopped to look me in the eye. We understood each other.

"Forget that powder. There are armed guards everywhere, even among the monks. No one can enter the shrine."

"There's a vent down there. A dog could get through."

"Yes, but there are dogs in the pagoda, Lara. Dobermans, bullmastiffs. They're guard dogs, trained by the monks."

"I'll take care of them."

"Huh?"

"Don't underestimate the power of a bitch in heat, Viskovitz." Her face was lit, sinful. Swinging her hips, she walked off toward the garden and showed herself to the pagoda dogs with her tail raised like a slut.

What could I do?

I whimpered a sutra and visualized a lotus blossom.

I saw her again three hours later. She smelled of all the dogs in the monastery, including Skittles. She was walking sideways and humming an old Cantonese song.

"Did you do it, honey?" she meowed. I took her outside the temple to my favorite hideout. An old house that was under construction and would never be finished. In a corner were three large bags. They looked like lime.

"Oh, Visko!" Her dilated pupils were as green as jade. "Come here. What are you waiting for?"

For just one night, one night, I forgot all the hardships of existence, the smell of rot, fleas. I managed to stop time, to dilate space and to reunite, on more than one occasion, with the Divine Stillness. It was finally dawn when I managed to detach myself. It had been a long day.

"Visko, I'd say that among all the dogs in the pagoda—"

"I don't want to hear about it," I growled.

"I love you, Visko."

"Don't say that, even as a joke. In a few days you'll be as cold as a squid, and it will be better that way."

"Can't you see that we're a perfect couple? You with your sense of smell and me with my dedication—"

"To duty? No, Lara. It's amazing how a few hormones always manage to deceive us. In this universe in which everything is unstable and ephemeral, nothing is more evanescent than love between dogs. No illusion is briefer. It is for this reason, I think, that we need other idols, other masters."

"Not you, Visko. You're not faithful to anyone. Not to the pack that raised you, not to the pagoda's monks, not to me. You don't have a master."

"You're wrong. I, too, have my leash, Lara. More painful than a studded collar. Sweeter than any other lie."

"Ljuba?"

"No." At that point, she might as well know the truth. I pointed to the fucking thing with my nose. Lara looked thoughtfully and shook her head.

"I don't understand. The powder? You enjoy confiscating it?"

How could anyone be so naive?

I tried to explain it to her. "Look, they put it under your nose from when you're a puppy—a hypersensitive nose like mine . . . day after day, at every fucking training session . . . well, your brain goes bazoom. Forget a little sugar lump or a little steak. Within a week you're its slave. And then nothing else exists in life. That's why I was so good at finding it when I was a cop: because I couldn't do without it. I certainly wasn't doing it to please the flatfoots who were drugging me . . ." I felt cold and was frothing at the mouth.

"I'll help you get out of it, Visko. My love is stronger. I would love you even if—"

"Even if what? Even if I told you that this stuff has been here for a week, since I dug it out of Korzybski's yard? Even if I told you that Korzybski died because he wasn't able to return the drugs to the Triad? Even if I told you that I killed Zucotic because he got in my way?"

"I don't believe it, I don't believe it, I don't believe it . . ." She was barking and backing toward the exit, with a bag in her teeth.

"Drop it, Lara!" I threw myself at her.

But just then two guys in uniform showed up, drawn by our yelping. Lara jerked herself free, leaving her collar in my teeth.

"You lose, Viskovitz," she barked as she ran to the officers for help.

How could anyone be so naive?

The two dogcatchers slipped a halter on her and dragged her into the van.

"What are you doing? Stop! I am Lara from Narcotics, Detective Lara reporting for duty. Detective Lara!" She really looked like a rabid dog, so dirty, so upset, without the pretty collar and the little tag.

I would never see her again.

I stayed there briefly, reflecting on the transitoriness of things. I had an urge to howl, but I checked myself, because this was Chinatown. I sniffed a little stuff and right away felt better. By then I was no longer sleepy, and I headed off for the pagoda.

Chinatown was waking up to a new day. On the sidewalks, young and old were doing the first tai chi exercises. The smell of ginger and onion was in the air, as was the far-off sound of the last saxophone. Everyone was busily returning to the harried rituals of existence, to performing the mystery of *Anicca,* the Great Illusion, the Dream of *Brahaman,* the Dance of Shiva, the Eternal Cosmic Joke.

The dogs of the monastery had begun their breathing exercises. I crossed my hind legs and assumed the lotus position. I concentrated on the *muladhara* to regain my energies and make them flow toward the place of salvation, beyond good and evil, pleasure and pain. Toward the heart of the life-giving pulse, toward the eye of clear wisdom, toward the Great Peace, the Great Peace . . .

How Low You've Sunk,
Viskovitz

"Ljuba, why don't you love me?" I asked.

"Because you're a worm, you're vile, you don't have a spine, you don't have any guts."

"And?"

"Because you're insipid. Because you have no head, no character, no sensitivity."

"And?"

"You don't know how to love, you have no heart."

"And?"

"You have a tiny penis."

"Anything else?"

"Yes, Visko. You don't ever think about me, you're an egoist, a parasite, you only know how to take, you live at my expense, you don't have an active life or interests, you're draining me, you irritate me all the time. When are you going to stop torturing me?"

A shudder of revulsion and disgust ran through her, shaking her whole body—then another and then another again.

To make it through the spasms I got a good grip with my scales on the mucus of her intestines. I wiped the blood off my proboscis and asked:

"And what would you say are my defects?"

BLOOD WILL TELL,
VISKOVITZ

"Papa, how did things go for you when you were little?"

"Childhood is the most wonderful time in a shark's life, Junior. My mother was a big fish, she nourished me splendidly. Naturally it took me a while to get her down, since I was so small, still in gestation. I started on the inside and made my way out through the blood-rich organs, so I can't say I really got to know her. I do remember she had a good heart."

"Were you an only child?"

"No, I had two brothers in the same litter. 'Visko,' they scolded me, 'now who will take care of us?' In those days

I couldn't stomach them. Then, when my stomach was empty, I took care of them myself."

"Didn't you suffer from loneliness?"

"Well, at a certain point I felt an emptiness. But to fill it up, there were uncles and aunts and cousins and grandparents. Family is in my blood, Junior. And friends helped me get along. I'd say everything went swimmingly until adolescence. Then I got my first remora."

"What kind?"

"The worst. I still remember his name—Zucotic."

"Did he make trouble for you?"

"Oh yes, you know what those creatures are like. They say they're symbiotic, but they're really parasitic. They fasten on to your stomach with those toothy fins and they don't ever let you go. But the worst thing is their hypocrisy. They criticize your every mouthful, they fill you with a sense of guilt. They tell you the personal history of every tuna and herring, so that when you eat them you lose your enthusiasm and the remoras get more leftovers. Son, I've seen remoras fatter than sharks."

"Couldn't you ask someone to pull them off?"

"Yes, but at that point I didn't have many friends. And Zucotic was basically my only company. You know, when you're young, an expert remora can even convince you he's helping you. But when I discovered I also had Petrovic and Lopez under my belly, I understood it was time to do something. I looked for a shark who could help me.

Someone who wanted to exchange the favor. That was how I met your mother, Ljuba."

"Did she have a lot of remoras?"

"So many you could only see her fins. And let me tell you, she wasn't small. Her pectoral fins were as big as rays, her anal fin supple as seaweed. Even her streamlined caudal peduncle made you stare. But above all it was her eye that struck you—red and set deep in the socket—mean as poison."

"Did you get along with each other right away?"

"Well, the first contacts were difficult, because remoras aren't stupid. They know how to recognize danger, and they don't think twice about sinking their whole set of teeth into your skin. But little by little, my parasites and hers felt a certain liking for each other. And then an outright affection. Consider that at a certain point my remoras were having their way with hers—and there she and I were, brushing our fins and gazing into each other's eyes."

"Couldn't you . . . I mean . . . after all . . ."

"Her remoras were mostly on her sex."

"And you couldn't pull them off her?"

"Certainly—but she didn't want me to. She had a terror of getting pregnant."

"Yes, of course. Like all female sharks."

"Anyway, at a certain point I'd had it with all this stalling, and I ate them off her. She returned the favor and a great love was born. Free of all restraints, our passion became frantic, Junior. We made love in the butchered bodies of whales, in the soft pulpy flesh of our prey. It was only by eating the flesh of others that we were able to keep from turning on ourselves. Throughout the deep we brought scandal and devastation, love and death, lust and loss. Naturally we couldn't hope to come through without so much as a scratch. So one day the water had a higher concentration of her blood than of her hormones. And at that point I had to get over her. It was while I was tearing her apart that I saw your little head stick out. Deep Ocean! You made me go all tender. Your dorsal fin was as small as a single scale. You were born prematurely, Junior, and that's why you came out so handicapped."

"But I'm not handicapped, Papa."

"Oh, yes you are. And it's my fault. It mustn't be nice for a kid to see the father tearing the mother apart and not even giving the kid a morsel. Loathing, sense of guilt, fear . . . you end up with a shrimp like you. Someone who grows up without any meanness, without blood lust. Just now I saw you playing around with that cod—why didn't you kill it?"

"I thought he was nice, Papa."

"You see . . ."

"There must be a way of living without hurting others."

"Sure—you live off me. Like a damned remora. Damn it, I've already explained to you that nothing does more good than evil. Around here the one critical standard everyone understands is our teeth. We're the ones who make this fucking ocean work. Is that clear? Imagine what would happen if every good-for-nothing was allowed to live without getting eaten."

"Maybe we'd all swim around more at ease, maybe we'd learn to respect each other."

"Respect is something you earn, kid, even from a herring. They know we kill them for their own good, and that's why they respect us."

"But—"

"But no one respects you, Junior. Look around. Tunas and mackerels are laughing at you. You're talking like a remora, you're behaving like a remora, you're even hanging on to my fin. You're becoming a parasite, goddamn it! The other day, when that female asked me, 'Want me to pull him off you?'—how do you think that made me feel? Her son is the same age as you, and he's already eaten up five or six baby-sitters. Don't you get it? I can't go on like this. Not if your name is Viskovitz."

"The thing is, I have other interests, Daddy."

"Right. Fooling around with blowfish and sea horses. Collecting diatoms. Listen to me: tonight Lara's coming to dinner with her daughters. Don't make us look bad, like that other time with those walruses. Or yesterday evening with those fishermen."

"Why? What did I do wrong?"

"You have more than three hundred teeth, Junior, I didn't give them to you so you could smile your silly smiles. I'm telling you this for the last time—you don't turn to whoever is next to you and ask demurely, 'Excuse me, could you pass me that drowned man?' You get a grip and tear, you cut and destroy, you pull stuff out of other people's gullets and you bite right into them. Have I made myself clear?"

"Even our dinner partners?"

"It's natural. For example, this evening it would be awfully nice if you cut up at least one of the babies."

"But they're the daughters of our guest!"

"Of course they are, you idiot. Nice people always bring something to help with the meal, it's polite . . . Look, here they are now. Don't forget—good manners . . . Hi Lara! Hey there, girls!"

"Hi Visko. And this is your little boy? Nice, nice . . . oh, oh, oh! These are the tuna you told me about? Oh, Visko, you shouldn't have . . . silver tunny . . . what a treat!"

"Yes, Lara. So hop to it, kids! Don't let them get away!"

"Aaarh. Gnarl. Chop. Growl. Ugh. Slash. Gasp. Squak. Yum."

"Thanks, Junior, for a wonderful evening. Your father was delicious."

"Your mother wasn't bad, either. Good night, girls."

You're Looking a Little Waxy, Viskovitz

Even as a larva I was rather attractive. "He's going to be a great drone," the nurses said more than once. "If this is the sketch, just imagine the finished work." Throughout the hive, my metamorphosis was viewed as an important social event, a big first. My antennae had barely emerged from the cocoon when there was a clamor of approval at the masterpiece. The critical reception was unanimous in appreciating "the chromatic liveliness, the solidity of the architectonic solutions, the refinement of the modeling." The interpretation was less unanimous. Some said, "What a posturing little drone! It's not the one with the tight abdomen or the sweetest setules who'll be the winner in the nuptial flight. You have to earn reproductive success with your head and your wings . . ."

"That could be," others replied. "But ours is a matriarchal society, and even if he's no genius and not exactly a lightning bolt with his wings, with a cute little ass like that, he'll go far."

The queen put an end to these sterile debates. Hers was the only opinion that mattered, and she made the most modern and courageous choice: Viskovitz.

But she had to make some concession to tradition, so on the eve of the nuptial flight she came before the honeycomb of the drones and announced, "She whom you see before you is Lara the Sweetness of the Poppy, by the grace of God and the pleasure of these combs your queen and sovereign. Tomorrow the sacred nuptial flight will take place. The start, as always, will be the shadow line cast by the ilex as soon as the sun makes an angle of sixty degrees with the hive. The rules of the contest remain the same: whoever takes a shortcut, stings a rival or makes two false starts will be disqualified and killed. And, as our Law decrees"—she let the gaze of her enormous eyes sweep over us—"whoever wins this trial will have his glory with me. May the best drone win."

I can assure you that as she said that, she wasn't thinking of Petrovic and Lopez. In reality it had already been discreetly set up that after the start, once the boys had swarmed off, she would meet me under the burnt oak.

I got a good night's sleep, and the next day I woke up in tip-top shape, as wired as a wasp. I ate a double ration of honey, licked my setules, shook my wings and went up to the starting line with all the suitors. I did a little warming up, a little stretching, and tried a few takeoffs. You can think what you like, but the nuptial flight is always a big day. The fans were all for Petrovic. Since he was the favorite, they had bet everything on him. I saw him buzz around nervously, chewing rosemary—a stimulant. At the start he reared up furiously, then took off and was in the lead right away. We all rocketed after him. Headed up at ninety degrees, he climbed through the curves, doing barrel rolls and zigzags to keep anyone from passing. It was too dangerous to try drafting because of the stingers. The rules? Nothing but words. Up here it was all buzzing, screaming and cursing. Pretty soon I had enough of that, and when we got away from the hive, I broke off and glided gently down to the oak and settled in a poppy.

She didn't keep me waiting.

"My hero," she gasped. "Take your glory with me!"

And I, Viskovitz, took my glory.

Later the sovereign declared, "Oh my knight, I like everything about you. Your palpiger, your submentum, your proboscis. Truly, beauty has your face and your name! I know that according to tradition I ought to castrate you and kill you, but this time will be a noble exception. In fact, I shall have to ask you to come live with me at court, I don't believe I can do without your body, your scent . . ."

"I see we understand each other. I have a certain need of that kind myself."

That evening I moved into the royal comb. The other males were proclaimed outlaws and exterminated. I honestly believe there was nothing I could do for them.

The life of a king was nothing less than I had imagined, and our honeymoon was very sweet. In the morning I got up late and breakfasted on royal jelly and precious pollens while the female workers curled my setules and stretched my wings. I soon became a father, and my chromosomes began to be mass-produced in a printing of five thousand copies a day.

But it wasn't all a bed of roses. One day I came back to the comb and found Lara curled up in front of the throne, weeping.

"The larvae, Visko. Every day I have to come up with five thousand names. You could at least help me."

"Let's call them all Viskovitz. Nothing wrong with that name. That way we'll have more time for us, my little star."

"Holy hives!" she exploded. "Is it possible that you're such an imbecile that you can't think past your own setules? And cover them up, damn it. And don't go around the hive with your wings spread out like that. The workers are female, after all. They're not getting any work done, the gatherers aren't gathering, the honey makers aren't making honey . . ."

"Well, it's hardly fair that the appreciation of beauty should remain the privilege of a small elite."

"Enough! Out of my sight!"

I decided that the time had come to move on. I'd never intended to be monogamous, after all. By nature I was meant to pollinate, to fly from flower to flower. I had always thought that cultivating and propagating beauty was my particular duty. It was in that spirit that I had always kept myself tanned and spritzed with cologne, making the effort to be—how shall I put it?—the artist, the work of art and its popularizer.

Promoting my image was easier than I'd thought. The courtesans arranged meetings with the queens and, day after day, my genes were being translated into new versions, put out in millions of exemplars. It was my apotheosis.

But the queens weren't used to sharing, and even the female workers began to ask for their turn. Diplomatic incidents and social tensions erupted. Even some wars, both between hives and between castes. My life became a hell.

So I decided to put an end to it. To make myself ugly. I slunk away to the underground passages where the solitary terricole bees lived, and I set about finding the nest of a certain Ljuba, a character who was known for her skill in reconstructive plastic surgery in wax. I was welcomed into an elegant waiting room lined in silk and waterproofed in the style of colletids, with resins and oily secretions. But when she came into the light . . . ah, I saw in her the very same misfortune that had befallen me: she was gorgeous.

She had the same "chromatic vivacity" in her setules, the same "delicate tracing" in her mouth parts, the same "curvilinear rhythm" in her filled-out body segments. In a word, she had what no other female in the ruches possessed: a personality. And notwithstanding that she had funds of honey and stores of wax, she was decidedly feminine and fully sexed.

"Good heavens!" she stammered as soon as she saw me. "They told me about you, but I really didn't believe . . ." She was overcome by the intensity of the moment. "That anyone could impart to a creation so much luminosity, such original effects of delineation . . ."

"Well, frankly, me neither. I didn't believe that . . ." I was overwhelmed as a little larva.

Damn, I said to myself, for the first time I'm meeting a bee who truly understands me, who can make sense of my beauty, and she's the very one I have to ask to disfigure me. I tried to explain the purpose of my visit.

"Aaaah," she moaned. "Don't talk heresy. I couldn't ever . . . When I operate on an insect, it's to make them look like you. And here you are, in your perfection, and you're asking me to . . ."

In the cells of her composite eyes there were thousands of images of me, and in mine, thousands of images of her. Each image of her reflected thousands of images of me which mirrored thousands of images of her in unison of visual ecstasy which reached far beyond fulfillment.

"Let's run away together, Visko. The world will be our honeycomb, life will be our nectar—"

"No, Ljuba. It would always be the same story. I know how cruel it is, but we must choose—beauty or life."

"Not now," she whispered. "For one night, let us celebrate their union."

"But Ljuba . . . we can't put into the world other creatures destined for unhappiness. With parents like us, their features . . ."

"You'll see. A little bit of wax can do wonders."

The next day she showed me. We pledged eternal love to each other, whatever masks life might make us wear. Then she showed how attached she was to me by making me so ugly that no other insect would dream of approaching me. With her prostheses of wax she transformed my cephalic parts into truly dismal scrawls and my whole face into an "insipid, opaque, rhetorically ornamented hotchpotch." In this way it was possible at last to fly around the meadows without being molested. I rediscovered the simple pleasures of life: love, work, family.

Ljuba oviposited in the spring, and I helped her forage for the incubating cells, watch over the brood, keep away predators and parasites. Life was peaceful, but I was still tormented by the thought of the wax. It was clear that we would have to put some on the little ones, too, or else folks would drag them off by their heels. The wax would work for a while, but what would happen when the summer heat melted our masks? It was already April . . .

One evening, as I returned to our underground passage, a grub announced, "They're born. They look like you."

"Like *me*?" I said, pointing to my waxy extensions. Certainly not *this* me, I said to myself. Like Ljuba, if anyone. I went down to the cells and looked them over. The grub was all too right. It couldn't be the wax, because they were still completing their pupal stage. They looked like *this* me. Like the implants I'd put on—they were glabrous, opaque, deformed.

"Ljuba!" I shrieked. "What the hell is going on? Who is the father of these monsters?"

"You are, Visko, I swear," she replied. Tears streaked her face, melting her waxy features, revealing her horrendous aphanipterous palps, even uglier than those of our young. I felt faint.

"Forgive me, Visko. I didn't have the courage to tell you . . . Come on, please, don't be like that. What really matters is being able to create beauty. Haven't we sworn to love each other, whatever disguises we have to wear? And which of us has more to complain about? You who only have to imagine my ugliness, or I who have to look at yours all day? I'll take care of everything, you'll see, even the kids will be okay. They only need a little . . . stylistic unity."

Before my very eyes she began to smear them with wax. In less than a half hour she managed to give them grace and dignity, to transform them into two rosy-cheeked baby dolls, appealing little fluff balls, children any parent would want to have, or at least see. I thought I was dreaming.

"Now, we mustn't make them cry or they'll melt," she warned. "You stay away from them with that waxy face of yours."

What could I do? They were a boy and a girl, and we named them Junior and Sherba.

I tried to convince myself that nothing had changed. After all, she was the bee who, more than any other, had known how to make me happy. And that was the only reality that mattered. But what would happen when the wax melted? I didn't dare imagine. If the kids were that ugly, even having a father like me, what must she look like? . . . It was already May.

One day, coming back to the comb, I idly stopped to watch a nuptial flight. There were six queens going off first, and I felt a pinch of nostalgia. I had found a spot facing the sun and, to finish up my errand, was extracting a little pollen from the flowers when I sensed that something wasn't going right.

Every sound had ceased and all eyes (composite or not) were on me.

Damn! The sun, I thought. It's melting my wax.

I got my wings whirring and took off like a rocket, but the queens, the six queens, were already on top of me. They began to pull at me, grabbing at my membranes, my setules, my antennae.

"I surrender!" I shrieked. "Don't pull me to pieces!"

They stopped with a start, astonished.

"Wax! He's covered with wax!" They wiped me clean with their spatulae and stared at me in a fury.

"What a lump! And he looked so interesting . . . but he's just another mannequin like all the others!"

Like all the others? It was only when I looked at the other drones that I understood. Not a setule out of place, not a single vulgar detail. They were all sons of mine. It was natural that they were identical to me. I was the father of the whole new generation, of the whole fucking nation. Even the female workers had my features. At this point, commonplace.

"Get rid of this imposter!" I was driven away with jeers and blows.

Ljuba was looking at me from a flower, snickering.

The sun was melting her wax, revealing all the monstrosity of her body and face. It came to me with a shudder that critical opinion would be unanimous in appreciating her "chromatic liveliness, the solidity of the architectonic solutions, the refinement of the modeling . . ."

You Look Like You Could Use a Drink, Viskovitz

"Papa, I want to stop drinking."

"Don't say such a silly thing, Visko. You're a sponge."

"What does that mean? That I have to spend my whole life stuck to this rock, filtering and pumping water like a vegetable?"

"You are a vegetable, Visko, or at any rate a zoophyte. How you go on . . ."

I despaired. All my attempts to create a life of swimming and pursuing my ideals were failing. Oh, if I only had muscles to push me to the calcareous sponge I loved and to merge with her into a single sycon! Oh, if I only had eyes to see her, a mouth to tell her I loved her!

All that I knew of my beloved were nitrogenous traces that the current carried to me. To those particles in suspension I had given a shape, pores and a name: Ljuba.

The one way to crown our love story was to reach her with some spermatozoa, but the current kept on running the wrong way—toward my mama, my sisters, my grandmothers, creating all kinds of family embarrassment and genealogical complications. The situation was rendered still more equivocal due to the periodic sex changes that we hermaphroditic sponges have to undergo. It wasn't easy for me to accept the fact that my father was the wife of his mother, that his daughter (my sister) was his grandfather and his grandmother was also his brother (my uncle). These relations were becoming even more morbid because of the way our bodies were piled together—it was difficult to figure out where you ended and where your immediate family began. And it wasn't easy to develop a healthy personality when the canals of your flagellate chambers were held in common with an invaginated mother, incestuous sisters and a bisexual father. When the only anatomical features on which you could construct an identity were the gastral cavity and the aperture of your osculum.

The tragedy of being a vegetable was that you couldn't commit suicide. The advantage of being a sponge was that you could drown your sorrows.

I prayed for something to happen. An earthquake, an ecological upheaval, that a cuttlefish would come to my rescue—something. And at last something did change.

The current. It reversed direction and finally put me in a position to fertilize the sponge I loved! I immediately turned my attention to wrapping my sperm in gemmules and beginning to fire them downrange.

But I didn't find any.

"Papa," I shrieked, "I'm sterile!"

"You're not sterile, Visko. You're a female. Like me."

I felt faint. How could I be so unlucky? Female. And meanwhile, Ljuba had become male, and her ejaculations couldn't reach me because I was upstream!

To add insult to injury, my mother's sperm began to rain down on me. And my sisters', and my grandmothers' . . .

"Damnation," I cursed. "Damnation!"

Even my daughter had gotten me pregnant.

I was my own mother-in-law. Damn it, my own mother-in-law!!!

But maybe it's all for the best, I sighed. Who knows? The way things were turning out, I might begin to hate the mother-in-law who was in me. Who can say that this unhappiness wouldn't finally make me happy?

THESE ARE THINGS THAT DRIVE YOU WILD, VISKOVITZ

What was left—I roared to myself—of our natural paradise, the Ngorongoro crater, the greatest in the world, the cradle of creation? Around me I saw only a movieland corrupted by nature show business. All that mattered was showing your fur and being talked about. And when did you get to be a success? Since the day I had appeared onscreen in a major role in a serial about great felines, I had become one of the park's stars, chased by cameramen, zoologists and zoophiles. I couldn't stand it any longer. I couldn't stand the entourage of chic beasts and snobbish ruminants, I couldn't stand hearing hyenas bark about dissolves and jump cuts. I needed a vacation.

A Thompson gazelle came up to me. A pretty, photogenic type, delicate, with withers measuring no more than sixty centimeters. Many starlets I knew would have been envious of her shiny coat, but she moved in a natural way; she didn't seem to be one of the usual soulless Lolitas. She asked me if I was Viskovitz the lion. Useless to deny it.

"I beg you, tear me to pieces."

"That can be arranged," I sighed. "But first you're going to have to audition."

"You didn't understand me. I'm being serious. Do you see this? It's a radio collar. Do you see these scars? They're from tranquilizer darts. And do you see these tags inside my ears? I have no peace, damn it!" She wasn't acting, she was really unhappy.

"I understand, dear. But I'm not the one you need to turn to."

"I'm very tender. I've always grazed on buds."

"I don't doubt it. But what you saw were documentaries, you don't seriously think—"

"What are those scavengers here for? Aren't they waiting for my leftovers?"

"Oh no." I smiled. "The hyena is Zucotic, he thinks he's my movie agent. The jackal and the lycaon, Petrovic and Lopez, are two extras. They always look like that."

"But surely there has to be a true wild beast somewhere," she mooed impatiently.

"Not in Ngorongoro. Here it's fashionable for carnivores to be vegetarian. Imagine what it would mean to tear apart live meat. Unless somebody ruins their close-up, of course. In that case, even an antelope would use its teeth. But I've heard that outside the crater, in the Serengeti, things are different, like in the old days. I suggest you try it there." I shook my mane in the direction of the Mandusi. "But watch out: you could like life in those parts."

With a sigh, she turned her snout. "Down there?"

"Yes. Beyond the lake there's a trail that climbs up to the crest. Ask once you get to the Seneto . . . In fact, you know what? I'll come with you for part of it, it'll be good for me."

We went through a small wood of fever trees and proceeded along the northern bank of the Makati to avoid the camping grounds, the landing strips and the lodges. In the meantime, I gave her advice that might come in handy in her new environment, if she ever came to cherish her life. I was telling her old stories about the Masai, poachers and white hunters, about the savanna that once was, when a lion's mane was still a king's crown and our roar was law. As I was doing that, my heart was beating fast and I thought I was seeing the crater of my childhood when, from the lake, there rose flights of flamingos, teals, ibises and curlews, marabou, spoonbills and jacanas. And in the Mandusi, hippopotamuses dozed under the eyes of the herons and nycticoraces, Jackson's widows and fantails.

The gazelle explained she wasn't leaving any loved ones

behind in those pastures. No one who was worth saying goodbye to. That she no longer had the herd instinct, since the chief gazelle had decided to abolish reproduction and put the species close enough to extinction to raise their value in the eyes of wildlife management. I was trying to comfort her, but I found myself complaining about the breakdown of the male feline's authority and the arrogance of lionesses who were growing more and more muscular, know-it-all, ambitious in a community—ours—that was becoming ever more similar to those of the hyenas, who had been living in matriarchal societies for some time now, and the results of *that* were there for everyone to see.

Laughing and joking, we reached the escarpment, and there I decided to follow her to the top to see what was on the other side: the Kilimanjaro, the Great Plains, Lake Victoria. A change of scenery, I explained to her, would do me a lot of good. We decided to stop near the crest. We ventured along a path that elephants and buffaloes had opened in the bushes and found shelter in a grove of nuxiae, gum trees and twisted junipers in the company of only a Cercopithecus and a few yellow baboons. There we stretched our legs and rested our heads on cassipurea moss. She was crying soundlessly, with quick sobs. I kept a paw on her shoulder and meanwhile wondered what it would feel like to sink my fangs in that slim neck and tear off pieces of that young, bleeding flesh. Probably a heaviness in the stomach, nausea and feelings of guilt, I said to myself. But maybe also a terrible pleasure . . .

"You smell good," she bleated all of a sudden.

"Pardon me?" My wandering paw had freed the odors from under my armpit: could she be mocking me?

"You have a nice lion smell, it's a masculine smell."

"M-m-masculine?"

"Yes. You lions are the most beautiful males in the savanna, so regal, so muscular . . . so much better than those effeminate herbivores. Have you ever asked yourself why all the ruminants have horns?"

"No, I—"

"You know, among us bovids there's almost no sexual dimorphism, and it always gave me the creeps, going with those guys." She turned toward me and languidly, wantonly, lowered her eyebrow ridge while the wind rippled her mane.

What could I do? Maybe it was the heat, maybe it was loneliness . . .

"Oh, Visko! It was marvelous!" she said afterward.

"Yes, it was good," I lied. It wasn't good. It was fantastic. There was more of the female in that little goat than there was in all the divas of my following put together, a pantheon of big cats who thought that pleasures of the flesh meant beefsteak. And I also liked that name of hers, Ljuba . . .

"It's a pity it can't last," she brayed.

"Huh? What do you mean?"

"What kind of a future could we have? We certainly can't stay hidden in these hills. Sooner or later we're going to have to go down to the plains. If we go down toward the Serengeti, someone will devour me. You're not the right age and don't have the necessary experience to defend me from those predators, it seems to me. But even if we got away with it, we would have to contend with the mentality of an environment that has remained more or less unchanged since the first day of creation, right? On the other hand, if we decide to go back, the situation won't be better: imagine what would happen once the media got hold of a story like ours. And then what kind of role models would we be for the young? It's one thing not to be racist, but between the species a certain distance is necessary. And anyway, even here we wouldn't be safe: don't forget, I have a radio collar, and sooner or later they would find us. Goodbye, Visko." She inhaled a tear, turned her tail and, swinging her hips, went down the hill toward the Olduvai Gorge and the Serengeti.

"Hey, wait a second, wait . . ." But she was already scampering down crags like a mountain goat. There was no way I was going to catch up with her. What could I do? I looked around. The view was breathtaking: for an instant I was suspended there, intoxicated by those wide spaces, those wild and boundless high plains that extended for hundreds of miles all the way to the Masai Mara . . . To my left I could see Ndutu and the flat savanna of Maswa. To the right, the Olduvai Gorge . . . my heart was beating like a cub's. Courage, old Simba, I said to myself. Who says you're too old for this life?

I took the path that led down to the valley and proceeded briskly alongside the road that led to the Naabi

Hill gap, to the Serengeti. When I went by, a crested crane, a secretary bird, bustards and wailing lapwings took flight. In these parts, being a lion still meant something.

I finally came onto an endless plain with short grass from which emerged the huge granitic formations of the odd Kopje. Thompson and Grant gazelles, zebras, black-tailed gnus, Jackson's elands, ostriches and oryxes grazed there under the watchful eye of cheetahs, lycaons, jackals and others of my kind. I couldn't help but admire the elegant dignity of those ruminants, and I surprised myself by letting my gaze linger on the curve of their rumps. A new sensitivity for certain simpler sights in nature had awakened within me: the slender necks of oryxes, steenboks, the speckling of kudus, the short coat of the impalas, the little tails of the dik-diks, the small asses on some of the giraffes. I don't know whether it was a survival instinct or modesty that made them move away with a certain alarm, murmuring and covering themselves with their tails.

I urbanely greeted some of the predators but didn't feel like asking for information. They had the lynx-eyed look of serial killers. Those guys didn't joke around: they tore things to pieces. And who knows what else they did to their prey that wasn't in any documentary. With a shudder, I thought of Ljuba.

For a week I trotted far and wide, moving carefully among those tall stalks, keeping a low profile so as not to irritate the proprietors of those territories, and finally I found her near the Kopje of Moru.

She was grazing with a group of small dik-diks and big sunis. She gave me a chilly reception, but I couldn't figure out the reason for her reserve. At any rate, she invited me to stay for the evening. She told me she had been adopted by the herbivores of that niche, that she had found a new family, new parents, new brothers and sisters.

"Come on, stay and eat with us," she bleated suddenly.

"I don't think that's a good idea, Ljuba," I objected. But she wouldn't listen.

"Mom? Dad? Guess who's coming to dinner!" She made way for me among a herd of bovids, and I followed her meekly, all purrs and good manners.

They tried not to betray any emotion, but they were struck dumb, as if bitten by a mamba.

I was introduced to two gazelles who talked to me with embarrassed coolness, and to two topis who simply looked at me with unconcealed aversion. I judged that the first two must be Mom and Dad, and the second two, dinner.

"*Jambo, habari gani? Mimi* Viskovitz," I said with the most politically correct roar I could muster, and I complimented the lady on the dinner.

It turned out I had been confused: the two gazelles were friends and the two topis were the adoptive parents. But by that point the faux pas was done and I had helped myself. For the entire rest of the evening we sat there looking at each other in embarrassed silence.

"Damn," Ljuba said later. "You told me you were a vegetarian."

"Yes, but I thought that here—"

"You see, I told you it couldn't last."

"Give me some time, Ljuba."

"No, Visko, we're too different, can't you see?"

I shook my head.

"And now I'm engaged."

With her muzzle she pointed out the two kids who were at dinner, one of whom was shaking like a leaf. "But it's not just that, Visko, you're old enough to be my . . ." She began counting. If she was one year old, there could be fifteen generations between us. "What can I say? We'd look ridiculous together, don't you see? And time won't make you any younger." She lowered her eyes.

It was there our story ended.

With my tail between my legs, I once again set out on the road past the caldera. She had hurt me. Not so much by what she said—basically she was right. But by the way she had said it. With a little twisted smile of compassion and embarrassment. I knew that feeling, I had felt it myself watching other animals undergo the humiliations of old age. When even the most cowardly animals made fun of them. When even the lowliest grip kicked them off the set because they were ruining the long shots. When even the tourists lowered their video cameras.

It gave me pleasure to see old friends again—the girls, the cubs. Even some hyenas.

Since that dinner, I never loved another ruminant. Or even ate one. Except that Ljuba, of course, or whatever her name was. For a little while, her fat made me gain weight, but with time and exercise *(roar)*, I worked it off.

You're an Animal,
Viskovitz!

I, Viskovitz, was a microbe.

I was told, "It's not size that counts, Viskovitz. The important thing is to be yourself."

As if that was easy. I'd barely had time to grow fond of my name when I became two microbes: VISKO and VITZ. Imagine what it was like when I turned into four: VI, SKO, VI, TZ. I was coming apart.

In the Precambrian period, we all were. Some said, "What can you do? That's life." I thought "metabolism" was a more appropriate word.

Our idea of fun was to become sediment along with

coacervates and proteinoids; methane and ammonia were considered a "nice atmosphere."

When I began to be called V,I,S,KO,V,I,T,Z, I saw it was time to do something. But what? And who would do it? I was in a minority even in myself. I was addressed as "they."

It was then that I heard the Voice: "V,I,S,KO," it said to me. "It's time to become an animal."

"Animal?" At that stage I was open to any suggestion— what was degeneration for one could be evolution for another. "I wouldn't know where to begin," we confessed.

"By being an egoist, by being full of yourself. We hold on to our little 'I' with all our might. It shouldn't be hard for you."

We tried. What was left of me in my eight microbes felt a tremor of pride, an increase of viscosity, and with a heroic effort, we molded them into one plasmodium. I believe that was the first multicellular organism, and was truly the first "I." To be precise, *I, Viskovitz.*

"And now?" I asked.

"Hmmm . . . Now you have to learn to kill and devour others. As big as you've become, that shouldn't be hard for you."

"Others who are alive?"

"Only until you've killed them, Visko. There's nothing wrong with it—it's called heterotrophic life."

It didn't seem dangerous. The life forms nearby looked pretty puny. I looked around and soon found some that fit the bill: Zucotic the bacillus, Petrovic the vibrio and Lopez the spirillum. Three septic and virulent paleogerms who'd been infecting me with their toxins for the whole Archeozoic era. I went up to them, slapped them around and ate them. It was the first instance of "survival of the fittest," a concept that would go far.

"And now?"

"Now you have to learn how to . . . do that thing. I mean to say . . . conjugate with another organism and recombine. Find someone you like and exchange some DNA."

"But—"

"There's nothing dirty about it, Visko. Follow your heart."

I thought he was referring to VITZ, the four cells who were kicking around in my sarcina—with a little imagination, you could consider them my heart. I ejected VI to see where he would go. He immediately began to wriggle away, taking off for the wide-open spaces, twisting and flexing his plasma. I followed him, paddling with my flagella until I saw him get to an albuminoid gelatin made of silvery microplasms, held together by long, filamentous cilia and purple fimbriae. That's where I lost his trail.

"Hey you, gel!" I yelled. "If I'm not mistaken, you've stolen my heart."

"Around here, hearts come and go," she sneered, the heart stealer. "What was yours like?"

"A spherical mycoplasm, somewhat flexible and squishy, the last time I felt it beat."

"Well, you can have it back if you want. But you're going to have to come get it, Plasmodium."

"Plasmodium is my morphotype. The name is Viskovitz."

"And gel is your aunt Sally. The name is Ljuba."

I cautiously moved alongside her and stuck to her gluey mass. Then I extroverted "I," stiffened him and sank him into her body so that he would find his lost partner. In the splish-splash I ended up losing "I" as well. He slid out of his membrane and dove, plasma and periplasma, into her "U."

And that is how I invented sex. I may have been a little clumsy, but my heart had been in it. I asked the gelatin how it had been for her.

"That's sex?" She burst out laughing, quivering all over. "You call that sex?" Still roaring with laughter, she contracted her siphon and took off without a backward glance, leaving me there with my heart in pieces.

It was the emptiness that hurt, that abyss in the center of my being. Not that VISKOTZ was an ugly name, you understand, but it was the name of a wounded Plasmodium, of a being maimed in its "I." I decided to build a cage of murein around the remains of my heart.

"Don't do it, Visko," the Voice warned me.

"You again!" I exclaimed. "Can we find out once and for all who the hell you are?"

"I am . . . the voice of your most ancient plasma. The primordial Microbe, the Protocell from which all of you were born, the I who includes all of you. You can call me VI."

"VI?"

"Yes, the VI. The VI of Visko, your mind; the VI of Vitz, your heart; the VI of the seed you sowed; the VI of all that is Vital, my son."

"Well, get a load of that." And yet that speech of his had a certain logic. Something of the first microbe might still be inside me. And inside the others. "So your plasma would be inside the whole lot of us? Even in that Ljuba, just to pick a name . . ."

"Exactly so. And I promise you one thing: you will find her again, Visko, you will find her again. And maybe things will go a little better. Maybe."

"And perhaps you were even inside Zucotic, Petrovic and Lopez?"

"Yes, and I still am. You'll be meeting them again, too, Visko. My imagination is what is."

"You'd like even those guys to evolve?"

"Not 'evolve.' That's a word I don't like. What is fun is 'change,' Viskovitz."

"Just a minute there. You called me Viskovitz. But you know perfectly well that name doesn't mean anything anymore."

"I know what I'm saying. Look into your heart and you'll see that I'm right. Go ahead, don't be afraid—it's not a spiritual exercise . . ."

I bent over, hydrolized my polysaccharides and peeked inside. Naturally I saw only T and Z. But then the V and the I of Visko began to stir. To copy themselves—they became bilobed, sectioned and finally split. A few minutes later the regeneration was complete, and I found myself face-to-face with him again—VITZ.

"Well, I'll be," I yelped. I was myself again, the old animal, in better shape than ever. Good, I said to myself. *Very* good. No one can stop me now. The time had come to teach the world a lesson. That thieving ecosystem! I burst out crying and laughing like a little kid. I was sure that from my salt tears, the ocean would take shape, yes sir, the ocean—and from there, life would begin, true life . . .

"Good for you," the Voice complimented me. "Now you're an animal. But you still have one more thing to learn."

"Let's hear it. Meiosis? Fermentation? Ontogenesis?"

"Death, Visko."

"You've got to be kidding."

"You're not a microbe anymore, Visko. Animals die."

"Just a minute, pal . . . give up everything?"

"Everything."